Acting Edition

A Twisted Christmas Carol

by Phil Olson

I0591855

SAMUEL FRENCH

FOR PRODUCTION INQUIRIES

UNITED STATES AND CANADA
info@concordtheatricals.com
1-866-979-0447

UNITED KINGDOM AND EUROPE
licensing@concordtheatricals.co.uk
020-7054-7200

Each title is subject to availability from Concord Theatricals Corp., depending upon country of performance. Please be aware that *A TWISTED CHRISTMAS CAROL* may not be licensed by Concord Theatricals Corp. in your territory. Professional and amateur producers should contact the nearest Concord Theatricals Corp. office or licensing partner to verify availability.

No one shall make any changes in this title(s) for the purpose of production. No part of this book may be reproduced, stored in a retrieval system, scanned, uploaded, or transmitted in any form, by any means, now known or yet to be invented, including mechanical, electronic, digital, photocopying, recording, videotaping, or otherwise, without the prior written permission of the publisher. No one shall share this title(s), or any part of this title(s), through any social media or file hosting websites.

For all inquiries regarding motion picture, television, online/digital and other media rights, please contact Concord Theatricals Corp.

MUSIC AND THIRD-PARTY MATERIALS USE NOTE

Licensees are solely responsible for obtaining formal written permission from copyright owners to use copyrighted music and/or other copyrighted third-party materials (e.g., artworks, logos) in the performance of this play and are strongly cautioned to do so. If no such permission is obtained by the licensee, then the licensee must use only original music and materials that the licensee owns and controls. Licensees are solely responsible and liable for clearances of all third-party copyrighted materials, including without limitation music, and shall indemnify the copyright owners of the play(s) and their licensing agent, Concord Theatricals Corp., against any costs, expenses, losses and liabilities arising from the use of such copyrighted third-party materials by licensees. For music, please contact the appropriate music licensing authority in your territory for the rights to any incidental music.

IMPORTANT BILLING AND CREDIT REQUIREMENTS

If you have obtained performance rights to this title, please refer to your licensing agreement for important billing and credit requirements.

A TWISTED CHRISTMAS CAROL had a rolling world premiere spanning eight cities beginning November 20, 2019. Those concurrent world premiere theatres/cities were:

Town Players, Watertown, South Dakota (opened November 20, 2019). The co-directors were Louis and Carter Canfield, the lights and sound were by Ryle Koistinen, and the set was by Sarah Henning and Marlin West. The cast, in order of appearance, was as follows:

DARLA JOHNSON	Amber Bosworth
BUFORD JOHNSON	Stuart Melby
BUBBA PICKFORD	Greg Dubois
DAISY NEWSOM	Sarah Henning
HANK WALKER	Delaine Nelson

High Desert Center for the Arts, Victorville, California (opened November 22, 2019). The production company was StageCrafters Productions, the director was Stephanie Brynjolfson, the stage manager was Jennifer Messer, the light coordinator was Marcella Terrasas, the set lead foreman was Michael Shaw, the producers were Michael Barrett and Sheila Fares, and the box office manager was Kristi Ehart. The cast, in order of appearance, was as follows:

DARLA JOHNSON	Sheila Fares
BUFORD JOHNSON	Steve Millikin
BUBBA PICKFORD	Russell Walkner
DAISY NEWSOM	Faith Kallenberger
HANK WALKER	Michael Barrett

Port Arthur Little Theatre, Port Arthur, Texas (opened November 29, 2019). The director was Richard Lene, the assistant director was Stacy Bradley, the technical director was Emerald Moreno, the set designer was Richard Lene, set artwork was by Molly Straw, properties were by Claudia "Kay" Lene, and the costumer was Jean Heubach. The cast, in order of appearance, was as follows:

DARLA JOHNSON	Stacey Bradley
BUFORD JOHNSON	Mark Bradley
BUBBA PICKFORD	Ben Porter
DAISY NEWSOM	Mayra Ceja
HANK WALKER	Carlos Sierra

Hill Country Community Theatre, Cottonwood Shores, Texas (opened December 5, 2019). The director, producer, lighting designer, sound designer, set designer, and costume designer was Mike Rademaekers, the stage manager was Helen Ward, the choreographer was Laura Gisi, and the box office manager was Louraine Robertson. The cast, in order of appearance, was as follows:

DARLA JOHNSON .... Christina Johnson
BUFORD JOHNSON .... Lew Cohn
BUBBA PICKFORD .... David H. Cowan
DAISY NEWSOM .... Ocean Leigh
HANK WALKER .... Michael Fox

Alton Little Theatre, Alton, Illinois (opened December 6, 2019). The executive director was Lee Cox, the artistic director was Kevin Frakes, the technical director was Brant McCance, the set design was by Kevin Frakes and Lee Cox, the lighting design was by Dennis Stevensen, the sound and special effects were by Brant McCance and Jake Tenberge, the stage managers were Logan Elliott, Kya Durie, and Helen Marmino, costumes were by Lee Cox, the production assistants were Lief Anderson, Patti Kruegel, Jenny London, Michael Cox, Ashley McAfoos, and the cast, the house manager was Linda Patton, the ticket manager was Michael Cox, volunteers were Diana Kay, and photos were by Vernon Hamel. The cast, in order of appearance, was as follows:

DARLA JOHNSON .... Mary Crank
BUFORD JOHNSON .... Kevin Frakes
BUBBA PICKFORD .... Brant McCance
DAISY NEWSOM .... Kim Hillman
HANK WALKER .... Loftin Wodiel

Main Street LIVE (formerly SCRT) Trinidad, Colorado (opened December 6, 2019). The director was Cora Warrick, the costume design, set design, and props were by Cora Warrick, the stage manager was Janna Remington, the set construction was by Fred Vaugeois, Danny Rubio, and Rene Vaugeois, the sound engineer was Fred Vaugeois, the lighting engineer was Danny Rubio, the production wardrobe was by Leisa Norris, the props/costumes were by Jeremy Montoya, and the artistic director and publicist was Kris Miller. The cast, in order of appearance, was as follows:

DARLA JOHNSON .... Barbara Privitt
BUFORD JOHNSON .... Louis Eodice
BUBBA PICKFORD .... Michael Lions
DAISY NEWSOM .... Nicole Burton
HANK WALKER .... Nathanael McCasland

Indian Valley Theatre, Sandwich, Illinois (opened December 6, 2019). The director was Connie Cline, the producer was Sharon Pagoria, the assistant director was Kyle Carr, the stage manager was Jen Ketchum, the assistant stage manager was Sam Miller, the set construction/master carpenter was Tony Pagoria, the lights and sound operations were by Darren Whaley, the lighting assistant was Nick Carlson, the publicity was by Sharon Pagoria, social media/photographer was Jen Ketchum, the program was by Sharon Pagoria and Kelly Gibbs, the flier design was by Lorali Curtis and Pete Pavia, costumes were by Paige Savage, Connie Cline, and the cast, and the box office manager was Ina Munar. The cast, in order of appearance, was as follows:

DARLA JOHNSON . . . . Melinda McGraw-Carpenter
BUFORD JOHNSON . . . . Tim Vogen
BUBBA PICKFORD . . . . Matt Savage
DAISY NEWSOM . . . . Drew Stralka
HANK WALKER . . . . Matt Frantzen

The Group Rep Theatre, North Hollywood, California (opened December 15, 2019). The director was Doug Engalla, the producer was Alyson York, the stage manager was Joseph Marcelo, the assistant director was Marc Antonio Pritchett, costumes were by Stephanie Colet, sound design was by Steve Shaw, set design was by Chris Winfield, publicity was by Nora Feldman, graphic design was by Doug Haverty, lighting design was by Kenny Harder, marketing/social media were by Kristin Stancato, and the artistic directors were Larry Eisenberg and Chris Winfield. The cast, in order of appearance, was as follows:

DARLA JOHNSON . . . . Lisa McGee Mann
BUFORD JOHNSON . . . . Van Boudreaux
BUBBA PICKFORD . . . . Christian Land
DAISY NEWSOM . . . . Veronica Roy
HANK WALKER . . . . Paul Cady

The alternates were Fox Carney (Buford), Jake Scozzaro (Bubba), and Bita Arefnia (Daisy).

CHARACTERS

DARLA JOHNSON – Strong-willed co-owner of a barbecue joint called "Buford's Open Pit Barbecue" who's been married to Buford for a long time.

BUFORD JOHNSON – Darla's husband. Strong-willed co-owner of Buford's BBQ. A Texan Archie Bunker.

BUBBA PICKFORD – Oblivious, dense business owner.

DAISY NEWSOM – Pretty, young, dreamy ex-short order cook at Buford's BBQ.

HANK WALKER – Famous barbecue legend, owner of Hank's Own Barbecue Sauce. A ladies' man.

SETTING

ACT ONE

Buford's Open Pit Barbecue, a little barbecue joint in rural West Texas, on Christmas Eve

ACT TWO

Same place, same time, moving toward Christmas Day

ACT ONE

(The play takes place in a small town in rural West Texas. It's Christmas Eve. The set is a local barbecue joint, "Buford's Open Pit Barbecue," with various Texas beer signs, a Texas flag, deer heads, longhorn steer antlers, and other West Texas barbecue joint trappings.)

(There are two tables with chairs around them. There's a photo of the owners, Buford and Darla, behind the bar. A Christmas tree is upstage by the front door. Wrapped presents and boxes of ornaments are under the tree.)

*(It's another slow day at Buford's Barbecue. As the lights go up, **BUBBA PICKFORD** is sitting on a barstool, drinking a beer, playing gin with **BUFORD JOHNSON**, who stands behind the bar. **BUFORD** is studying his cards. **DARLA JOHNSON** is decorating the tree, enthusiastically singing "Deck the Halls" in her highest voice, a capella.)*

DARLA.
DECK THE HALLS WITH BOUGHS OF HOLLY,
FA LA LA LA LA LA LA LA LA.
'TIS THE SEASON TO BE JOLLY,
FA LA LA LA LA LA LA LA LA...

BUFORD. *(Annoyed.)* ...Darla!

DARLA. Yeah, hon.

BUFORD. Could ya please keep it down?

DARLA. Okey dokey.

> *(Singing enthusiastically, in a much lower-pitched voice.)*

DECK THE HALLS WITH BOUGHS OF HOLLY,
FA LA LA LA LA LA...

BUFORD. ...Darla!

DARLA. Yeah, hon.

BUFORD. Do you know, "The Sound of Silence"?

> **(BUBBA** *picks up a card.)*

DARLA. *(Reacts.)* Come, sing with me.

BUFORD. No, thank you.

DARLA. *(To* **BUBBA.***)* We used to have karaoke night here. Buford would sing me love songs.

BUFORD. That was a long time ago.

DARLA. I just love Christmas. It's such a magical time.

BUFORD. Yeah, watchin' all my money magically disappear.

DARLA. Oh, you. How would ya like to help me decorate the tree?

BUFORD. Oh, sure, puttin' hot lights on a dead tree. Might as well just throw lighter fluid on it.

DARLA. It's plastic, ya doofus.

BUBBA. Is it startin'?

DARLA. Every year. Go ahead, there, Buford. Get it all out.

BUFORD. I'm tellin' ya, it's just another Hallmark holiday that got outta control. I mean, the whole thing about spendin' money on presents, and then havin' to be nice to people, and then ya gotta go to church.

DARLA. One day a year won't kill ya.

BUFORD. It killed Jesus.

DARLA. Buford!

BUFORD. Oh, I'm jokin'... The thing is, Christmas is for the children. Well, if ya had a husband that could give ya one, maybe we could enjoy Christmas, but ya don't, alright, so why don't we just go ahead and skip it this year.

(**BUBBA** *goes behind the bar.*)

DARLA. I told ya a million times, that's not important to me.

BUBBA. *(Opening a beer.)* C'mon, Buford. You don't need children to enjoy Christmas.

BUFORD. *(Sarcastic.)* Just go ahead and help yourself, there.

BUBBA. *(Oblivious.)* Alrighty, thanks.

BUFORD. Don't you have a gas station to run?

BUBBA. I got six gas stations, and I'm off today.

BUFORD. You're off every day.

DARLA. Oh, come on, Buford, where's your Christmas spirit?

BUFORD. It's in the liquor cabinet.

BUBBA. *(Laughs.)* 'Cause liquor is a spirit. I get it. Sure 'nuff, y'all.

(*Holds his two hands out like he's shooting two revolvers.*)

Pa chow.

DARLA. Remember when ya used to love Christmas?

BUFORD. *(Looking at* **BUBBA**.*)* I can't remember the last time we had a payin' customer.

BUBBA. *(Chuckles.)* That's funny. Sure 'nuff, y'all.

> *(Holds his two hands out like he's shooting two revolvers.)*

Pa chow.

> *(**BUBBA** takes a drink of beer.)*

BUFORD. What's with the, "Sure 'nuff, y'all"?

> *(Holds his two hands out like he's shooting two revolvers.)*

Pa chow.

BUBBA. It's my new catchphrase.

BUFORD. Well, that's unfortunate.

BUBBA. It's positive and it includes everybody.

DARLA. When do ya use it?

BUFORD. Do not encourage him.

BUBBA. Tourists come into one of my stations, buy some gas, I throw 'em a "Sure 'nuff, y'all."

> *(Holds his two hands out like he's shooting two revolvers.)*

Pa chow… They buy an extra heat lamp chili dog with their purchase, maybe a pickled egg. That's called an "upsale." Booya!

BUFORD. Why are you here?

BUBBA. Just passin' by.

BUFORD. Well, the next time ya pass by, please do.

DARLA. C'mon, Buford, be nice.

BUFORD. What are we, Baptists?

DARLA. Oh, lighten up, would ya? 'Tis the season to be joyful.

BUFORD. Be joyful for what, huh? We never have any customers, we barely make the mortgage payments on this place. Be joyful for that?

DARLA. I'm not complainin'.

BUFORD. Yeah, well ya should, alright, and I'll teach ya how.

DARLA. You're the expert.

BUFORD. That's right.

(**DARLA** *starts wiping down the table.*)

DARLA. If we need more money, I can always go back to work at Kramer's Pharmacy.

BUFORD. Oh, no. No wife of mine is gonna work... Ya missed a spot there.

(*He points to the spot.* **DARLA** *shoots him a look.*)

I'm the breadwinner, and I wear the pants in the family.

BUBBA. And Darla controls the zipper.

(**BUFORD** *shoots him a look.*)

Look, Buford, if ya need money, I can put ya to work in one of my gas stations. I got six now. Sure 'nuff, y'all.

(*Holds his two hands out like he's shooting two revolvers.*)

Pa chow.

BUFORD. Do you have an "off" switch?

BUBBA. No, but I can hold my breath for one minute in my bathtub.

BUFORD. (*Thinks.*) Well, thanks for plantin' *that* image in my head.

DARLA. At least Bubba is happy. Maybe you could learn somethin'.

BUFORD. What is *he* happy about? His fiancée ran off to Amarillo with that plywood salesman. Yeah, I said it, and there ya go.

BUBBA. Oh, c'mon there, Buford. You's just not in the right frame of mind. They's must be somethin' ya like about Christmas.

BUFORD. Can't say there is.

BUBBA. Everybody loves Christmas. C'mon, what do y'all want this year from Santa?

BUFORD. I want you to hold your breath for four minutes in your bathtub.

BUBBA. But I would die.

BUFORD. Darn it.

DARLA. C'mon, Buford, tell us what Christmas means to you. Don't be a chicken.

> (**BUBBA** *and* **DARLA** *start making chicken noises, clucking and flapping their wings.*)

BUFORD. Alright, enough from the two French hens!... Here's what Christmas means to me: it's the one time of year that reminds me of what I *don't* have.

DARLA. Well, ya have *me* and that's all ya need.

BUFORD. Yeah, well...

DARLA. Tell me ya love me.

BUFORD. Oh, come on, Darla, I told ya I loved ya when we got married. If anything changes, I'll let ya know.

DARLA. Husband of the year.

BUBBA. I'll be over here, keepin' score.

BUFORD. Oh, you know how I feel about ya.

DARLA. Remind me. How do you feel about me?

BUFORD. *(Thinks.)* Warmly.

DARLA. *(To BUBBA.)* And that's the key to our relationship; honest communication.

BUFORD. I have never lied to you.

DARLA. Really? Is my sister prettier than me?

BUFORD. *(Stunned by the question.)* No. Yes. This is entrapment!

DARLA. See?!

BUFORD. Well, if ya don't want me to lie, stop askin' me questions.

DARLA. I'm just askin' for a little communication.

BUFORD. When ya communicate, ya just get in trouble, alright. The less you say, the fewer mistakes you're gonna make. So keep it in, bottle it up, and no one gets hurt.

DARLA. Worst advice, ever.

BUFORD. It's just how I am, alright. It's how I grew up. My dad was like that and my parents have been married forever. I don't see what the big deal is.

DARLA. Well sometimes change is good.

BUFORD. Oh, come on, it's not like *you* don't have any flaws.

DARLA. Okay, you're right, I admit that sometimes I wake up grumpy... Other times I let him sleep in.

BUBBA. *(Laughs.)* Oh, a zinger!

DARLA. I'll be here all week. Try the brisket.

BUBBA. One point for Darla. Sure 'nuff, y'all.

(Holds his two hands out like he's shooting two revolvers.)

BUBBA. Pa chow.

BUFORD. If it wasn't for marriage, men would live their lives thinkin' they had no faults at all.

BUBBA. Oh, you don't really mean that.

(To **DARLA.***)* Buford loves ya, Darla, he'd take a bullet for ya,

(To **BUFORD.***)* wouldn't ya?

*(***BUFORD** *thinks, doesn't answer.)*

Wouldn't ya?

BUFORD. Like, what kinda gun, like a BB gun?

BUBBA. No.

BUFORD. A pellet gun?

BUBBA. No, a real gun. With a real bullet.

BUFORD. Ya mean, like it grazes me?

BUBBA. No.

BUFORD. Maybe hits me in the butt?

BUBBA. Would you die for Darla?

BUFORD. Would the death be permanent?

DARLA. Oh, just forget it.

BUBBA. Buford, you's a lucky guy to have someone like Darla. When I first met Darla, I thought you was holdin' her against her will.

BUFORD. Yeah, I know.

BUBBA. I mean, some of us thought that Darla was your "make a wish."

BUFORD. Alright, I get it. I know. Darla was a real catch back in the day. She won that County Fair Rodeo Queen contest when we first met. She was beautiful.

DARLA. "*Was* beautiful"?

BUFORD. That's right, you were.

DARLA. "*Was* a real catch"?

BUFORD. I'm tryin' to compliment ya here, okay?

DARLA. "Back in the day"?

BUFORD. You're welcome.

BUBBA. Hey, Buford, why don't ya give Darla an early Christmas present. That'll lighten things up.

BUFORD. Yeah, alright, good idea. I got somethin' right here for ya.

(He grabs a card from the Christmas tree and hands it to **DARLA.***)*

Here ya go.

DARLA. *(Underwhelmed.)* It's a card.

BUFORD. Go ahead, open it.

*(***DARLA** *opens it.)*

DARLA. *(Reading.)* "Merry Christmas to the person that I live with."

(To **BUFORD,** *unimpressed.)* Wow.

BUFORD. Best part's comin' up.

DARLA. *(Reading.)* "You are the catfish to my trout. You are the Bass to my Crappy." *(Pronounced "crap-pee.")*

BUFORD. That's pronounced, "Crappie." *(Pronounced "crop-pee.")*

DARLA. No, this is crappy. Ya didn't even sign it.

BUFORD. That's so I can return it.

DARLA. Return it?

BUFORD. Yeah, and get ya another one next year.

DARLA. *(Sarcastic.)* I am so hot for you right now.

BUFORD. You are?

DARLA. No!

>   *(She hands the card back to **BUFORD**.)*

BUFORD. Oh, c'mon, we're on a budget.

>   *(**BUFORD** puts the card back under the tree.)*

DARLA. *(To **BUBBA**.)* Buford's so cheap, he won't even pay attention.

>   *(Looks at **BUFORD**, who is not paying attention.)*

(*To **BUBBA**.)* Isn't that right, Buford.

BUFORD. *(Startled, he looks at her.)* You say somethin'?

DARLA. I rest my case.

BUFORD. Oh, I get it. You're still mad that I taped over our wedding video. I said I was sorry, but Texas Tech was playin' the Horn Frogs.

BUBBA. You still have a VCR?

DARLA. He's cheap.

BUFORD. Alright, fine, I'll get a dvd player. I saw one at the Goodwill for five bucks.

DARLA. It's not that, I just wish that you'd surprise me sometimes.

BUFORD. Like how?

DARLA. Oh, I don't know, bring me flowers for no reason.

BUFORD. Honey, when a man brings his wife flowers for no reason, there's a reason. And believe me, I have never had a reason to bring you flowers.

　　　　(Thinks about that.)

That sounded better in my head.

DARLA. I give up.

BUBBA. Now don't fret, Darla, I can fix this. Okay, we're gonna do a little marital exercise I call, "touchy feely."

BUFORD. I will "touchy feely" my foot in your butt.

　　　　(DAISY enters, carrying a cookie tin.)

DAISY. Hey, y'all, merry Christmas!

BUBBA. *(Opens his arms for a hug.)* Daisy!

DARLA. Hey, you're back!

　　　　(DAISY walks past BUBBA's outstretched arms to DARLA.)

DAISY. *(Hugging DARLA.)* Hey, Darla.

　　　　(Hands the cookie tin to DARLA.)

These are for you.

DARLA. *(Opening the tin.)* Oh, you are so sweet.

　　　　(DARLA eats. BUFORD grabs one and eats it.)

DAISY. I call 'em, "Daisy's fried ham poppers." I made 'em myself.

DARLA. Oh, wow, these are good.

BUBBA. I'll have one.

　　　　(DARLA ignores BUBBA, putting the cookie tin on the bar.)

BUFORD. *(Likes the poppers.)* Not bad.

DAISY. Thank you.

BUBBA. I'll have it later.

DARLA. *(To DAISY.)* You wanna beer?

> *(DARLA gets DAISY a beer.)*

DAISY. Sure, it's noon somewhere.

> *(DAISY goes to hug BUFORD.)*

Hey, Buford.

BUFORD. *(Putting his hand up, stopping her.)* Not a hugger.

DAISY. Oh, that's right. I forgot.

> *(DAISY takes a step back. BUFORD holds up his fist. She touches her fist to BUFORD's.)*

BUFORD. There ya go.

DARLA. *(Sarcastic.)* That's all *I* get.

BUFORD. Well, why don't ya just tell everybody about our "romantic" life.

DARLA. It's a short story.

BUFORD. Hardy har har.

DAISY. Hey, Bubba.

BUBBA. Hey, Daisy. You're lookin' good.

> *(He holds his arms out for a hug. DAISY doesn't go for it. He puts them down.)*

DAISY. Thank you. So are you.

BUBBA. *(He blushes.)* I know. I got six stations now. "Mach tach lah kalonach..." That there's "six" in Klingon. I'm takin' the Rosetta Stone.

DAISY. Good for you.

BUBBA. You smell good. You wearin' somethin' special?

DAISY. Soap.

BUBBA. Well, that's some mighty fine smellin' soap. Sure 'nuff, y'all.

> *(Holds his two hands out like he's shooting two revolvers.)*

Pa chow... That's my new catchphrase.

DARLA. What was the old one?

BUFORD. Do not prolong this.

BUBBA. The old one?

> *(Gesturing a billboard.)* "If y'all need gas...I got some."

DAISY. Well, *that* I knew.

BUFORD. So, how was the "big city"?

DAISY. Oh, it was good. I got a job waitressing at the Bigfoot Lounge in Amarillo. Some times they let me make appetizers. I tried to get a job as a sous *(Pronounced "Sue.")* chef, but that didn't work out.

BUFORD. What in the corn muffin is a sous chef?

DAISY. It's what I did here before I left.

BUFORD. You were a short-order cook.

BUBBA. I don't know why you wanna go to Amarillo to cook. I mean, you can do that right here.

DAISY. 'Cause they got more restaurants there, and it's what I wanna pursue.

BUBBA. Why?

DAISY. What do ya mean, "why"?

BUBBA. Well, what's the big picture? Where ya gonna go with it?

DAISY. Well, some day I'd like to be a famous chef at one of them fancy restaurants like the Olive Garden. Maybe have my own cookin' show on TV in front of a live audience like Rachael Ray.

BUBBA. Pretty tall order for a short-order cook.

*(He laughs. **DAISY** shoots him a look. He corrects himself.)*

Sous chef.

DAISY. Well, ya gotta dream big, or don't dream at all.

DARLA. Amen.

BUBBA. So...how's the plywood salesman?

DAISY. Oh, well, we're not goin' out anymore.

BUBBA. *(Perks up.)* Say what?!

DAISY. Yeah. That didn't really work out.

BUBBA. Really?

*(He turns and does a little victory dance to **BUFORD**. He turns back to **DAISY**, busted. He composes himself.)*

Sorry to hear about that.

DAISY. I don't know, I just can't seem to find the right guy.

DARLA. Well, keep lookin'. You'll find him.

BUBBA. *(Raises his hand.)* He's right here.

DAISY. *(Ignoring **BUBBA**, to **DARLA**.)* Yeah, but where?

BUBBA. *(Still holding up his hand.)* Here.

DAISY. What do you say, Darla? How do ya find the person that's right for you?

*(**BUBBA** drops his hand in frustration.)*

DARLA. Ya better ask Buford. He's much better at choosin' a partner than I am.

*(***BUFORD*** contemplates that.)*

DAISY. *(To ***BUFORD***.)* When do ya know when you're ready to get married?

BUFORD. Simple. When you can no longer dress yourself or speak on your own behalf.

BUBBA. I know it's hard to believe, Daisy, but I am available.

DAISY. Oh, Bubba, let's not go through all that again.

BUBBA. But I'm a different person. I'm funny now. I've been writin' jokes. Okay, here's one I've been workin' on...

(He takes out a piece of paper and reads.)

What do you call a bull with one horn?

DAISY. I give up.

BUBBA. *(Thinks for a beat.)* That's all I got so far. It's a work in progress.

DARLA. So, what are your plans?

DAISY. Oh, yeah...umm... I wanted to talk to you about that. See, I was wonderin' if maybe I could get my sous chef job back.

BUFORD. *(Correcting her.)* Short-order cook.

DAISY. Just 'til I get back up on my feet.

DARLA. Sure 'nuff, y'all!

(Holds her two hands out like she's shooting two revolvers.)

Pa chow.

BUFORD. Darla, we can't afford to have...

(Speaking Pig Latin so **DAISY** *won't understand her.)*

BUFORD. "Aisy-day ack-bay."

DARLA. We can, too. We have "uh-nee-may" in the "avings-say."

BUFORD. And that's why they call it the, "avings-say."

DARLA. He still has his first "ickel-nay."

DAISY. What if I do a live cookin' show right here for a percentage of beer sales? Then if I get folks in, it's like a commission.

DARLA. That's a great idea!

BUFORD. No, it ain't.

DAISY. How 'bout this, Buford, if I don't double your business in the next three weeks, you can fire me.

BUBBA. If you came in here once a week, you'd double their business.

BUFORD. Hey, Bubba, come here, would ya?

(He grabs a bar towel.)

I'm gonna stick this in your mouth.

*(***BUFORD*** goes after ***BUBBA***.)*

BUBBA. Oh, come on, Buford, it's Christmas.

*(***BUBBA*** runs into the kitchen.)*

BUFORD. Yeah, I got your present right here, little drummer boy.

*(***BUFORD*** follows ***BUBBA*** into the kitchen.)*

DAISY. I don't know how you and Buford do it.

DARLA. It's called, "combat compatibility."

DAISY. What's that?

DARLA. The ability to fight with each other and still get along.

DAISY. Well, they say that marriage ain't a sprint, it's a marathon.

DARLA. I ran a marathon once. I was only happy when it was over.

DAISY. Oh, it can't be all that bad.

DARLA. It wasn't that bad in the old days 'cause ya died when you were, like, forty. Now ya live till you're ninety. I mean, when they thought up the whole "till death do us part," we weren't in it for that long.

DAISY. Ya ever think about motivational speakin'?

DARLA. Oh, it's not all bad.

DAISY. See, I knew it.

DARLA. When you're in love and ya get married it's the most glorious two and a half hours of your life.

> (**BUBBA** *comes out of the kitchen.* **BUBBA** *is wearing a hat with mistletoe hanging from it just above his face.*)

DAISY. What in the tarnation is that?

BUBBA. It's mistletoe.

DAISY. Take it off, Bubba.

BUBBA. Just one kiss. C'mon, it's Christmas.

DAISY. You're embarrassin' yourself, now take it off.

BUBBA. Oh, all right.

> (**BUBBA** *quickly takes the hat off and sticks it in his front belt, completely oblivious of what he's doing. The mistletoe hangs over his crotch. He has no idea.*)

DAISY. You need counseling.

> (**DAISY** *grabs the mistletoe hat from* **BUBBA**'s *belt and puts it on the bar.*)
>
> (**BUFORD** *comes out of the kitchen.*)

How about it, Buford? I could use the work.

BUBBA. Daisy, I got a deal for ya. You know how much I care for ya, right, and I know ya need money so, I'll give ya fifty bucks right now if ya give me a kiss.

DAISY. Bubba, there's a word for someone who does that kind of thing for money.

BUFORD. Yeah, "wife."

> (**BUFORD** *laughs.*)

DARLA. Excuse me?

BUFORD. Instantly I regret sayin' that.

DARLA. Is that what you think of me?

BUFORD. What?! No, I just... Have you lost weight?

DARLA. Would you like my mother to move back in with us?

BUFORD. Honey, it was a joke. It's just that we don't have enough customers, we're strapped for cash right now.

BUBBA. I know what you need to get more customers, a new catchphrase. Here's one:

(Gesturing a billboard.) "Food...that you can eat."

BUFORD. I don't need a catchphrase.

BUBBA. *(He takes out his cell phone.)* How about a new name for the place. I just don't think "Buford's Open Pit Barbecue" is workin' for ya.

BUFORD. It's workin' just fine.

BUBBA. *(Looks at his cell phone.)* Well, ya need somethin'. Let's see what people are sayin' about ya on the Yelp.

BUFORD. Do not look at those reviews.

BUBBA. *(Looking at his cell phone.)* Oh, boy, y'all got one star. Whoa.

BUFORD. Put that away.

BUBBA. This guy calls ya "Buford's Arm Pit Barbecue."

BUFORD. I'm warnin' ya.

BUBBA. "Buford's barbecue sauce tastes like a steamin' pile of –" Dang, is that even a word?

(**BUFORD** *makes a move toward* **BUBBA.**)

Puttin' it away, puttin' it away.

BUFORD. Those idiots don't know a thing about barbecue.

BUBBA. It's all about the sauce, and I know just what you need. You need to start usin' Hank's Own Barbecue Sauce.

DAISY. Oh, my gosh, Hank's Own Barbecue! I love that sauce. I put it on my pancakes.

BUBBA. Best darn barbecue sauce in the world.

BUFORD. Do not mention that guy's name in here.

BUBBA. Who? Hank Walker?

BUFORD. I said don't mention – have you got no seeds in your pumpkin?

DAISY. You're not still jealous of him, are ya?

BUBBA. Come on, Buford. Darla only dated Hank for a couple months.

(*To* **DARLA.**) What did y'all say, "He's a good business man, and that's about it."

BUFORD. Don't you have a gas station to run, or six.

(*Mocking* **BUBBA.**) "Mach tach lah kalonach."

(Holds his two hands out like he's shooting two revolvers.)

BUFORD. Pa chow.

DARLA. Buford, we've been through this. You have nothin' to worry about.

BUFORD. Then why do you keep bringin' him up?

DARLA. I'm not bringin' him up.

BUFORD. Yeah, well, not out loud, okay, but you think about him. Telepathically. I know, you do. I bet you sit there every day with your little antennas up, wonderin' what your life would be like if you married the "great" Hank Walker.

DARLA. Are you through?

BUFORD. He could probably give ya a baby, there, too.

BUBBA. What, you ain't got no buckshot in the old rifle?

BUFORD. Bubba!... I got buckshot, alright? They're just a little slow, that's all. Like you.

BUBBA. Oh, ya got the lazy tadpoles.

DARLA. When Buford was in high school he stepped on a rake. Took one hard in the...

(Motions where he got hit.) Jingle bells.

BUBBA. Oooo, that'll make ya sing soprano.

BUFORD. Alright, ya know what, first of all, I am all man, okay? One hundred percent bull moose manly man.

*(**DARLA** laughs.)*

I'm sorry?

DARLA. Allergies.

BUFORD. Second of all, can we not talk about my...man business?

BUBBA. So, is they just slow or is they dead?

BUFORD. What did I just say?

DARLA. He had a checkup last week. We're waitin' on the results.

BUFORD. Oh, come on, Darla, that's private.

BUBBA. Well, I'm rootin' for ya, Buford.

BUFORD. See what ya did, there, Darla? Bringin' that up. I didn't wanna checkup anyway. Doctor makin' me do stuff I don't wanna do.

BUBBA. I know what your problem is. You wear them tighty-whities. You're stranglin' 'em.

I wear them Duo Tang long johns with the freedom pouch… Oh, and they got that escape hatch for emergencies… This one time after eatin' three burrito supremes I was out in the woods, and I just, down she goes.

(**BUBBA** *motions like he's pulling down his pants.*)

DAISY. Do you have any boundaries at all?

BUBBA. I will *not* go to Lubbock.

DARLA. Better quit while you're behind, Bubba.

BUBBA. I'll say this, if you're tryin' for a baby, you better hurry. I mean, the older you get, the riskier it is.

DARLA. Yeah, I know I'm getting up there, Bubba. Thanks for remindin' me.

BUBBA. Oh, Darla, stop, you ain't gettin' up there.

DARLA. *(Smiles.)* Thanks.

BUBBA. You's already there.

DARLA. *(Turning on a dime.)* I will end you!

DAISY. Have you got no grain in your silo?

BUBBA. Why don't ya try that in vitro test tube baby deal? I hear they can make them super babies with x-ray vision and mind control.

BUFORD. Or she can just go back to Hank Walker.

(**BUFORD** *heads for the door.*)

DARLA. Where ya goin'?

BUFORD. I'm fixin' to go four-wheelin' down by Willow Creek.

DARLA. It's Christmas Eve, Buford.

BUFORD. And when I come back, I'm takin' down the Christmas tree.

DARLA. Well, then don't come back!

BUFORD. Fine!

DARLA. Scrooge!

BUFORD. (*Thinks of a comeback.*) Martha Stewart!

(**BUFORD** *leaves.* **DARLA** *storms into the kitchen.*)

BUBBA. What in the Sam Houston was *that* all about?

DAISY. I reckon that Buford's still mad at Hank Walker.

BUBBA. Why? Darla only dated him for a couple months.

DAISY. You don't know about the barbecue sauce?

BUBBA. What barbecue sauce?

DAISY. Buford never told ya?

BUBBA. He don't tell me nothin'.

DAISY. Before Buford met Darla, he owned a barbecue food truck with Hank Walker. They were partners. Buford created this barbecue sauce that everybody really liked, and they were doin' real well. But then they had a fallin' out, Buford left the business, Hank took his sauce, called it "Hank's Own Barbecue Sauce," sold it to stores, it makes a ton of money and Buford opened up *this* place.

BUBBA. So, Buford didn't get no money for the barbecue sauce?

DAISY. No. He couldn't prove that he created it.

BUBBA. Don't he have the ingredients?

DAISY. He wrote 'em on a piece of paper, gave it to Hank and Hank said he "lost it." He tried, but he's never been able to duplicate the recipe.

BUBBA. Oh, jeez, well, that's just awful…

(Turning on a dime.) Anyway, back to me. Remember the first three times I proposed?

DAISY. *(Thinks.)* Yeah, Bubba, I remember.

BUBBA. We might could do that again, ya know.

DAISY. Oh, Bubba, I need to pursue my restaurant career and you want me to stay home. I just can't do that.

BUBBA. Yeah, but, ya see, ya won't have to cook 'cause I'll take care of ya. I mean, you won't never have to work again. That ain't so bad, is it?

(DAISY doesn't budge.)

Oh, Daisy, sweetie…ya know that warm feelin' ya get when ya accidentally light yourself on fire?

DAISY. *(Thinks.)* No.

BUBBA. I want that feelin' again… With you.

DAISY. Yeah, that's a hard pass.

BUBBA. Please.

DAISY. No.

BUBBA. Please.

DAISY. No.

BUBBA. Please.

DAISY. No.

> *(**BUBBA** leans in to kiss her.)*

What are you doin'?

BUBBA. *(Backs up.)* Oh, I'm sorry, I was gettin' mixed signals from ya.

DAISY. Language is not your first language, is it?

BUBBA. Well, your words is sayin' one thing and your actions say the same. It's confusing.

DAISY. Bubba, it's just not gonna happen, okay, hashtag, not a chance.

BUBBA. Oh, I see. Playin' hard to get, there. Alright. Alright. Well, two can play at that game, there, missy. Oh, yeah, you're on. You are on. I'm gonna walk right out that door, right there. That door that I'm pointin' to, alright? And then you'll be sorry. Oh, yeah, you will. Just try to stop me, too. Yeah, I said it, go ahead, just try to stop me.

> *(She doesn't.)*

Seriously, try to stop me.

> *(She doesn't.)*

Okay, well, then just forget it, alright? I ain't gonna give ya your present, then, okay, 'cause it's a good one.

> *(She doesn't flinch.)*

Alright, I will, but I ain't wrappin' it!

> *(**BUBBA** leaves. **DARLA** comes out of the kitchen and gets a beer for **DAISY**.)*

DARLA. Sounds like Bubba still has some feelin's for ya.

DAISY. Yeah, I reckon.

DARLA. I guess I never figured out why you were with Bubba in the first place.

DAISY. Well, land sakes, it ain't like I had a lot of options or nothin'. I mean, Bubba was the only single guy in town, and maybe he did get off the boat before it reached the dock...but he is crazy about me. And he was generous, and protective, and he took me places and stuff.

And my parents couldn't afford to send me to the El Paso Hair Institute so I don't have a fancy education. I mean, at least he offered me a nice lifestyle. That's somethin' I never had.

DARLA. So, what ever happened to the plywood guy, then?

DAISY. Oh, I don't know. I wanted a cookin' career, and he just wanted to drive Miss Daisy.

       (**DARLA** *sits next to* **DAISY** *on a stool.*)

DARLA. *(Nods.)* Oh...

       (Thinks.)

Yeah, I don't know what that means.

       (**DAISY** *whispers something to* **DARLA** *in her ear.*)

I don't know what that means either.

DAISY. Don't matter... So, you and Buford still at it, huh?

DARLA. Oh, yeah.

DAISY. You'll get through it. Ya always do.

DARLA. I called my mom.

DAISY. Oh, yeah? How's she doin'?

DARLA. Oh, she's fine... I'm gonna move in with her.

DAISY. Oh, you say that *every* year.

DARLA. Yeah, well this time I'm serious, alright? I mean, things were good when we got married. He was real nice and thoughtful and stuff, but then he just changed into this bitter angry guy, gettin' all jealous of Hank Walker, and insecure about his man business, and I'm just tired of it, alright? I mean, I feel like I'm just spinnin' my wheels.

DAISY. Have ya talked to him about it?

DARLA. I try to talk to him, get him to open up, and share his feelin's with me. I even suggested couples therapy.

DAISY. Ooh, how did that go over?

DARLA. He just stared at me, all glassy-eyed. It was like... his wheel was turnin', but the hamster was dead.

DAISY. Bubba's wheel hasn't turned for three years.

DARLA. It's so dang simple. He'd have me back in a heartbeat if he just knew that all I want for Christmas is love.

> (**DARLA** *goes to hang ornaments on the tree. Just then,* **BUBBA** *runs into the bar.*)

BUBBA. Buford's in the hospital!

> (**DARLA** *turns to* **BUBBA.***)*

DAISY. Oh, my gosh. Is he alright?

BUBBA. Oh, yeah, he's fine...he's just in a coma.

> (*In semi-shock,* **DARLA** *starts taking ornaments off the tree.*)

DAISY. What?! What happened?!

BUBBA. I don't know. I didn't get a lot of details.

DAISY. Oh for, why the heck not!

BUBBA. Well, it didn't happen to *me*!

DAISY. *(Groans.)* Ohh...

> (**DAISY** *sees* **DARLA** *taking ornaments off the tree.)*

What are ya doin', Darla?

DARLA. He'll come back. I just have to take the tree down. That's what he wanted.

DAISY. She's in shock. Darla, Buford's in a coma.

DARLA. He'll be fine. We'll just skip Christmas this year.

DAISY. *(To* **BUBBA.***)* We should go see him.

BUBBA. Yeah, we should.

DAISY. Darla, let's go see Buford, okay?

DARLA. Yeah, alright.

> (**DARLA** *continues to take ornaments off the tree.)*

DAISY. Darla, hon, let's go see him, *now.*

DARLA. Sure, alright... I need to get somethin' at the drug store, anyhow.

> (**BUBBA** *leads her out the door.)*

We'll take the tree down, later.

> *(They all exit. Just then, the lights flicker, and a strange, dream-like sound is heard.* **BUFORD** *enters from the kitchen, wearing a hospital gown, with an Ace bandage wrapped around his head. He looks a little like Scrooge did when he wore his nightclothes.)*

BUFORD. Where in the Bird's Eye frozen peas is all the beef jerky? Darla, we got any more beef jerky? Somebody ate it all... Darla?!... Oh, for, ya want somethin' done, ya gotta do it yourself.

>   (**HANK WALKER** *enters from the bathroom, wearing a tuxedo, carrying a glass of Scotch.*)

HANK. *(Singing, in his best lounge-singer voice.)*
JINGLE BELLS, JING-JINGLE BELLS,
JINGLE ALL THE WAY.

>   *(Seeing* **BUFORD.***)* Buford Johnson!

>   (**HANK** *goes to hug* **BUFORD.***)*

BUFORD. *(Puts his hand up to stop him.)* Don't hug me... That's just awkward.

HANK. Buford, it's me.

BUFORD. Hank Walker?!

HANK. The one and only.

BUFORD. What are *you* doin' here?

HANK. Well, let's just say I'm kinda your tour guide.

BUFORD. Yeah, well, the only tour you're gonna take is out that door, okay?

HANK. Whoa, hey, what's with the attitude?

BUFORD. Oh, don't you play dumb with me, now.

HANK. I'd never win.

BUFORD. That's right.

>   (**BUFORD** *realizes what he just said.*)

HANK. Oh, yeah, you're mad about the barbecue sauce. Right... Well, *you* stole my woman.

BUFORD. So, what are you here to steal her back, then?

HANK. No, not at all. Actually, I'm here to help ya.

BUFORD. Oh, yeah, that's a laugh.

> *(DARLA, DAISY, and BUBBA enter the bar.*
> *DARLA is upbeat.)*

Oh, there you are. Hey, Darla, look who the weasel dragged in.

DAISY. The doctor says he moved his little finger. That's somethin'.

BUFORD. *(Looking at HANK.)* Yeah, well, he's movin' more than that... Wait, what?

DARLA. He says there's not a lot of brain activity, but we already *knew* that... Anyone wanna beer?

> *(BUBBA raises his hand. DARLA goes to get*
> *some beers.)*

BUFORD. Alright, I get it, you're still mad at me. Whatever.

(To HANK.) She's ignorin' me.

HANK. They can't hear ya, Buford.

BUFORD. Sure they can. Come on, Darla, the game's over.

DAISY. Why don't we finish the tree, Darla? Take your mind off it.

DARLA. Take my mind off what?

BUFORD. Yeah, take your mind off what?

DAISY. Off Buford gettin' hit by that twister.

DARLA. Oh, yeah.

BUFORD. I got hit by a twister?

DARLA. I told him not to go four wheelin'.

BUBBA. They say that twister just came outta nowhere, rolled his pickup three times. Ended up in the creek.

DAISY. Good thing he was wearin' his seat belt.

BUBBA. Y'all think he'll come out of his coma?

DARLA. *(Sadly.)* They were not optimistic.

(Turns to happy.) I just love Christmas.

BUFORD. Oh, for cryin' out loud.

BUBBA. *(Holds up a beer.)* I'd like to propose a toast. Whatever happens to Buford, in order to preserve his legacy, I shall take his pickup truck.

> **(BUBBA** *drinks.)*

> **(DARLA** *and* **DAISY** *go to put ornaments on the tree.* **BUBBA** *goes to help them.)*

BUFORD. Alright, first of all, Bubba, you're a bonehead. If I go, I'm takin' my pickup. Second of all...

(To **HANK.***)* I'm in a coma?!

HANK. You heard 'em.

BUFORD. So...what is this like a dream or somethin'?

HANK. Yeah, sort of a cross between a dream and... Judgement Day.

BUFORD. Well, who's the judge?

HANK. *(Looking up, talking to God.)* Uh-huh.

(To **BUFORD.***)* One point off for not knowin'.

BUFORD. Oh, for Pete's sake.

BUBBA. Excuse me, ladies. I gotta go see a man about a euphemism.

> **(BUBBA** *goes to the bathroom.)*

DAISY. Hey Darla, ya got any deep-fried pork nuggets?

DARLA. Yeah, in the kitchen.

> **(DAISY** *goes into the kitchen.)*

BUFORD. So, what are you like a guardian angel or somethin'?

HANK. If I'm an angel that would imply that you're goin' to Heaven.

BUFORD. Wait a minute. You're alive, though, right?

HANK. Yeah, I'm really just kind of a dream-slash-Judgement Day messenger.

BUFORD. Okay, well, it was nice talkin' to ya, there, haircut. I'm gonna just go ahead and wake up now.

(Slaps his face.) Alright, here we go, wake up, wake up, come on.

HANK. Actually, ya got a fifty-fifty chance.

BUFORD. They got odds in Heaven?

HANK. *(Laughs.)* Again with thinkin' you're goin' to Heaven.

BUFORD. So Darla thinks I might die?

HANK. That's right.

DARLA. *(Sings and dances as she goes into the kitchen.)* JOY TO THE WORLD, THE LORD HAS COME.

BUFORD. She don't seem too broke up about it.

HANK. Can ya blame her?

BUFORD. Ya know what, it don't really matter, alright? 'Cause this is just a nightmare from eatin' some bad catfish, and tomorrow I'll wake up, and there ya go.

HANK. I guess I forgot to mention the little test ya gotta go through first.

BUFORD. Test? What kind of test?

HANK. Oh, I don't know, think of it like a driver's test to see if you're worthy to go back on the road.

BUFORD. It took me three times to pass the driver's test.

HANK. Ooh. This is harder, too. Bummer.

BUFORD. Okay, just tell me what I gotta do, alright? Let's just get this thing over with.

HANK. Okey dokey. Now, before tomorrow mornin', you'll be visited by three spirits, the ghost from Christmas past, present and yet to come. If ya get through it, you might live.

BUFORD. So I just gotta make it through the scary ghosts, then?

HANK. That's it.

BUFORD. Alright, then. Let's get this barn dance started. Where's the first ghost?

(Looking around.) Come on, let's go, where are ya? Bring it on!

> *(**HANK** makes ghost sounds, shaking a little tiny chain.)*

HANK. Oooooooooooooooooh.

BUFORD. That's about as scary as a rodeo clown.

HANK. Well, they *are* kinda scary.

BUFORD. Oh, yeah, you're right. They are.

> *(**DARLA** comes out of the kitchen as the **DARLA** she was eight years ago. She has her hair in a ponytail, and a different shirt.)*

DARLA. Hey, Buford, how do ya like my new shirt?

BUFORD. How much did it cost?

> *(**BUBBA** comes out of the bathroom, wearing a fake beard.)*

BUBBA. It looks great, honey. Of, course you would look good in a beer label.

BUFORD. What in the chimichanga is this?

> (**BUBBA** *and* **DARLA** *do a cheesy Eskimo kiss with their little cat paws out.*)

BUBBA & DARLA. Mew, mew, mew, mew, mew, mew, mew.

BUFORD. Get off her!

HANK. That's you eight years ago in your Christmas past.

BUFORD. Me?... That's Bubba with a fake beard.

HANK. Budget constraints.

DARLA. Sweet cheeks, will you give me a foot massage?

BUBBA. You know I will, snuggle muffin.

> (**DARLA** *sits in a chair and takes off her shoes.*)

DARLA. I just love your foot massages.

BUBBA. Not as much as I love givin' 'em to ya.

> (**BUBBA** *starts massaging* **DARLA**'s *feet.*)

BUFORD. *(To* **HANK.**) I gave Darla foot massages?

HANK. You sure did.

BUFORD. I must have blocked that out.

DARLA. *(Re: the massage.)* Oh, that feels so good. Oh, yeah, oh, yeah.

BUFORD. That's disgusting.

BUBBA. Ya like that?

DARLA. Oh, I love it. Oh, oh, ohhhhh!

BUFORD. Stop that!

HANK. Ease up, Buford. It's just her feet.

BUFORD. And feet lead to ankles...

DARLA. I am in hog heaven.

BUBBA. This little piggy went to market.

DARLA. *(Laughs.)* Oh, you are so funny.

BUBBA. Oink, oink.

DARLA. *(Laughs.)* Oh, you.

BUFORD. That's just stupid.

DARLA. You're the best husband I ever had.

BUBBA. You're the best wife.

BUFORD. Why are you showin' me this?

HANK. To remind ya what it used to be like.

BUBBA. I wish I could be a better provider, huggy bear.

DARLA. Oh, sugar loaf, all we need is each other.

BUBBA. I know, but if I could just remember that barbecue sauce recipe, we could get more customers, and bring in more money so I could buy you the things you deserve.

DARLA. You want me to go and talk to Hank Walker about gettin' the recipe back from him?

(**BUFORD** *shoots* **HANK** *a look.*)

BUBBA. No, I don't, cuddle bunny. Hank Walker is a celebrity, who I look up to, and he shouldn't be bothered by the likes of us.

BUFORD. Okay, I *know* I never said that.

HANK. Creative license.

DARLA. You'll figure out the recipe, my little cabbage patch.

BUBBA. I hope so, butter dumplin'.

(**BUBBA** *stops rubbing* **DARLA**'s *feet.*)

DARLA. Thank you for the foot massage, spinach dip.

BUBBA. You're welcome, my little gravy bowl.

(**DARLA** *puts her shoes back on.*)

BUFORD. Oh, for rice cakes.

BUBBA. I love you more than football.

DARLA. I love you more than spanks.

BUBBA. I'd die for you.

DARLA. *(Thinks.)* You win.

(**BUBBA** *and* **DARLA** *do a cheesy Eskimo kiss with their little cat paws out.*)

BUBBA & DARLA. Mew, mew, mew, mew, mew, mew, mew.

BUFORD. Stop that!

HANK. They're just showin' affection.

BUFORD. We never expressed that much love for each other.

HANK. That's for dramatic effect.

BUFORD. There's no way we were ever that happy.

HANK. Yeah, you were.

BUFORD. Well, we ain't now.

HANK. Why?

DARLA. Oh, Buford. I've never been happier in my life.

BUBBA. Me neither. I love you more than Bubba is stupid.

(Thinks, "I'm Bubba.") Wait.

DARLA. Why don't we adopt?

BUFORD. Oh, here we go.

BUBBA. No, no, no, you know how much that costs? Let's keep tryin'. I can do it. 'Cause I'm a manly man.

BUFORD. The manliest.

DARLA. You wanna baby, don't ya?

BUFORD. Yeah!

BUBBA. More than anything.

DARLA. I have a surprise.

(Yells toward the front door.) Come on in!

> *(Through the front door comes* **DAISY** *on her knees with a little wooden crutch, wearing a hat, hiding her hair, smiling, happy. She has boots on her knees, like Tim Conway playing "Dorf." She's Tiny Tim.)*

BUBBA. What in the tuna melt is that?

DARLA. He's an orphan.

BUFORD. That's Daisy with boots on her knees.

DARLA. He's up for adoption.

BUBBA. I don't want somebody else's kid. Especially not a little ragtag street urchin.

DAISY. *(With a proper British accent.)* You want some of this? Bring it on, Twinkle Toes.

DARLA. Come on, Buford. Give him a chance. He's very talented, and he's clean.

BUBBA. What's his name?

DAISY. Thanks for asking. You can call me Tiny.

BUBBA. Alright, whatcha sellin'?

DAISY. If you would consider adopting me, I could move out of the orphanage and get off the streets.

BUBBA. Streets build character.

DARLA. Buford, just hear him out.

BUBBA. Alright, for the sake of argument, let's say I would consider adoptin' you, which would require an investment of considerable size since you probably eat food and whatnot. Why should I invest in Tiny? Give me your best elevator pitch. Go.

DARLA. Oh, Buford.

DAISY. That's okay. I'll give it a go. If you let me stay, I'll be very quiet. You won't even know I'm here, and I'll work for you, for free.

BUBBA. "For free"? You have my attention.

DAISY. I'll do the dishes, take out the trash, wash and wax your pickup, I even do windows.

DARLA. *(To BUBBA.)* Huh? Huh?

BUBBA. I'm listenin'.

DAISY. I can cook, mow the lawn, clean the restaurant, and when you're old, I will change your diapers.

BUBBA. *(To DARLA.)* Change my –

DARLA. Well, *I'm* not gonna change 'em.

DAISY. I don't eat much, and I never complain.

DARLA. *(Baby talk, to DAISY.)* Oh, you just wanna hug him.

BUBBA. No, ya don't.

DAISY. And I can tell jokes. Knock, knock.

BUBBA. *(Reluctantly.)* Who's there?

DAISY. Hanna.

BUBBA. Hanna who?

DAISY. *(Singing, a capella.)*
HANNA PARTRIDGE IN A PEAR TREE.

(DARLA laughs.)

BUBBA. Where's my gun?

DARLA. Oh, Buford.

DAISY. I'm a good dancer. I'll dance for you for food.

(She dances.)

DAISY. Big finish, here we go!

> *(***DAISY*** does a big finale, then takes a bow.)*

DARLA. *(Applauds.)* That was great.

> *(To* **BUBBA.**) What do ya think?

BUBBA. I think he'd be good on "America's Got *No* Talent."

DAISY. Please sir, if you don't adopt me, I will cry.

BUBBA. Cryin' is good. It cleanses the pours.

DAISY. Please don't send me back to the orphanage. They'll beat me.

BUBBA. Don't take this the wrong way, Tiny, but...we just don't wantcha.

DARLA. Oh, Buford!

DAISY. That's okay. I'll just finish the dishes, and when I'm done I'll take out the trash, then hobble to the bus station, where I'll probably get mugged.

> *(***DAISY*** starts toward the kitchen.)*

BUBBA. Make sure ya put the lid on the can. We got raccoons.

> *(***DAISY*** goes into the kitchen.)*

DAISY. *(As she exits, crying.)* Waaaaah! Waaaaah!

DARLA. How could you be so mean?

> *(***DARLA*** storms into the kitchen.)*

BUBBA. It's not so hard. I was raised Lutheran.

> *(***BUBBA*** follows her.)*

BUFORD. So, what ever happened to Tiny?

HANK. Tiny went to Hollywood, joined a boy band, got hooked on the crack reefer, and hasn't been heard from since.

BUFORD. Why are you doing this?

HANK. I told ya. To help you.

BUFORD. "Help me" do what?

HANK. Help ya pull your head outta your butt, 'cause if ya don't, you're gonna die a lonely, bitter man.

BUFORD. Oh, listen to you. The guy who made me bitter.

HANK. Oh, get over it. You got more important stuff to worry about than me.

BUFORD. Yeah, like what?

HANK. Like Darla. Have ya ever talked to her about your feelin's?

BUFORD. Nothin' good comes out of talkin', alright. It just leads to arguin', and then gun play.

HANK. Darla just wants ya to open up to her.

BUFORD. And then what? A movie? Dinner? Flowers? Ya do one thing for 'em, the bar keeps gettin' raised higher and higher.

HANK. Do you have any idea what Darla really wants from you?

BUFORD. Oh, gosh, let me think. A better lifestyle?... A baby?... You?

HANK. You have no idea.

BUFORD. Here's an idea. I know why you're here. To steal my woman.

HANK. I am not. Ya know what, you're as stubborn as a red-headed prom date named Shirley.

(**HANK** *reflects on his prom date with Shirley.*)

BUFORD. Alright, ya know what, get outta here. Right now.

HANK. I'm tellin' ya, you're gonna lose your wife if ya don't make some changes.

BUFORD. I don't need to change. I'm doin' just fine, thank you.

HANK. That's your problem, Buford, you're not doin' fine. You're just too thick to know it.

BUFORD. Hit the bricks, bow tie. Get out of my dream-slash judgment day.

HANK. No, can do, Peter Pan. You're only one-third of the way home. You still got Christmas present and Christmas yet to come.

BUFORD. Yeah, well, I don't care about that stupid Christmas yet to, whatever, alright? Now, get outta here.

HANK. I think you might regret it.

BUFORD. *(Pointing to the bathroom.)* There's the exit, SpongeBob.

HANK. Ya know, if you're not careful, you're gonna manifest what you believe.

BUFORD. *(Still pointing to the bathroom.)* Go!

HANK. *(Sings "O Christmas Tree" with his best lounge-singer voice as he exits through the bathroom.)*
O TANNENBAUM, O TANNENBAUM,
THAT'S "CHRISTMAS TREE" IN GERMAN.

(To audience.) Thank you.

> *(HANK exits. Just then, DARLA and BUBBA come out of the kitchen, wearing the same things they wore at the beginning. DARLA has some mail in her hand.)*

BUBBA. Maybe we can go visit Buford again in a little bit.

DARLA. *(Sarcastic.)* Yeah, whatever.

> (**DARLA** *goes behind the bar and looks at the mail.*)

BUFORD. Oh, that's nice... Alright, so, what, are we in Christmas present, now?

HANK. *(Popping his head out of the bathroom.)* Yes.

> (**HANK** *goes back into the bathroom.*)

BUBBA. Christmas just ain't gonna be the same without Buford.

DARLA. No, it won't... It'll be better.

BUFORD. Oh, that is high-larious.

> (**DARLA** *holds up an envelope, looking at it.*)

DARLA. Looks like we got the doctor's results on whether or not Buford can "provide" a baby.

BUFORD. What does it say?

BUBBA. Open it.

BUFORD. No, don't. I don't wanna know.

DARLA. Without Buford, it don't really matter anyway, now, does it?

BUBBA. Ya know, Darla, I know things are tough right now and you're probably not registerin' what's goin' on yet, but I just wanna say that Buford's been under a lot of stress lately and sometimes he says stuff to overcompensate as a defense mechanism for his own insecurity... I saw that on *Dr. Phil.*

BUFORD. Is that right? Tell us less.

DARLA. He's been sayin' stuff like that for eight years.

BUBBA. *(Insincere.)* Yeah, well, I tried.

BUFORD. Nice effort.

> (**DAISY** *comes out of the kitchen in normal clothes.*)

BUBBA. Hey, I think we should open up a present before dinner.

> (*He reaches under the tree and picks up a small ring box.*)

Oh, look. Here's one from me to Daisy.

> (**BUBBA** *holds the ring box out to* **DAISY.**)

DAISY. Oh, yeah, see, umm, no, no, no, no, no.

BUBBA. What's wrong?

DAISY. That's a ring box.

BUBBA. How do ya know?

DAISY. It's the same one from the first three times ya proposed.

BUBBA. Well, maybe it's not a ring. Maybe it's somethin' else.

DAISY. Is it somethin' else?

BUBBA. I was just sayin', "Maybe."

DAISY. Yeah, alright, Bubba, why don't ya just go ahead, there, and put that away for now.

BUBBA. "For now." Still in the game!

> (**HANK** *enters, still wearing his tuxedo.*)

HANK. Hey, y'all! Merry Christmas!

ALL. (*Except* **BUFORD.**) Merry Christmas.

BUFORD. I thought I told you to leave.

HANK. Darla?... Darla Streelund?

BUFORD. It's Johnson now. She's married!

DARLA. *(Lights up.)* Gracious sakes, it's Hank Walker!

    *(***DARLA** *hugs* **HANK**.*)*

DAISY. Hank Walker! As I live and breathe, it's Hank Walker! The barbecue king!

BUBBA. Now don't get your panties in a bunch.

DAISY. Too late...oh, my gosh, I'm gonna faint. Somebody catch me.

    (She gestures to **HANK** *to hold her up.* **BUBBA** *goes to* **DAISY**.*)*

    (To **BUBBA**.*)* Not you.

BUFORD. *(To* **HANK**.*)* They can see you?!

DARLA. What are *you* doin' here?

BUFORD. Yeah!

HANK. I was just passin' by, thought I'd stop in and say howdy.

BUFORD. Howdy. Now leave.

HANK. Ya look great, Darla. A vision to behold.

DARLA. *(Blushes.)* Oh... And you look like...Robert Goulet.

HANK. It's the moisturizer.

    (To **DAISY**.*)* And you're Daisy.

DAISY. He knows my name. Oh, my gosh, he knows my name.

    *(***HANK** *hugs* **DAISY**.*)*

He's huggin' me. Ohh.

BUFORD. He's workin' the room!

HANK. I had your fried ham poppers at the Bigfoot Lounge in Amarillo.

DAISY. You had my poppers?! Well, butter my biscuits!

BUBBA. *(Raising his hand.)* I volunteer.

HANK. You're a good cook.

DAISY. He said I'm a good cook! Hank Walker said I'm a good cook! I'm gettin' the vapors!

BUBBA. Alright, hold your horses there, Kemosabe.

HANK. And you're Bubba. You own those gas stations.

BUFORD. He inherited 'em.

HANK. What do ya call 'em?

BUBBA. *(Gesturing a billboard.)* "Bubba's...Gas."

HANK. Great name. Powerful.

BUBBA. Took me a year to think of it.

HANK. I bet. I hear you got the best heat lamp chile dogs in West Texas.

BUBBA. Put some hot sauce on 'em. Sure 'nuff, y'all!

> *(Holds his two hands out like he's shooting two revolvers.)*

Pa chow.

HANK. Love the catchphrase. It's positive and it includes everybody.

BUFORD. Brown nose.

BUBBA. *(Hands **HANK** a business card.)* Here's my card. It'll get ya five percent off on grape Slurpees.

DARLA. Can ya stay for dinner? We have an empty place at the table.

> *(**DARLA** gestures to a chair at a table.)*

BUFORD. Wait, what?! No, that's *my* place!

HANK. Sure. I'd love to.

DAISY. Sweet December. Hank Walker is stayin' for dinner.

BUFORD. *(To* **DARLA.***)* What are you doin'?

HANK. So, where's your husband?

DARLA. Who?

BUFORD. Me!

HANK. Your husband.

DARLA. Oh, yeah, right, umm...he's dead.

BUFORD. No, I'm not!

BUBBA. Actually, he's in a coma.

BUFORD. Thank you for the upgrade.

DARLA. When I said "'til death do us part," I didn't realize I was settin' a goal.

(**DARLA** *and* **HANK** *laugh.*)

HANK. Oh, Darla.

DARLA. Too soon?

BUFORD. Well, yeah!

HANK. That's too bad about your husband. I'd like to see him. It's been a long time.

BUFORD. Ya just saw me ya knucklehead!

DARLA. Can I get you a beer?

HANK. You bet.

(**DARLA** *goes to get* **HANK** *a beer.*)

BUFORD. She don't miss me at all.

HANK. *(Affectionately.)* Oh, Darla, what ever happened to us?

DARLA. Oh, I don't know. I got married to, ah, starts with a "B"...

> *(DARLA thinks.)*

BUFORD. Buford!

DARLA. Buford.

DAISY. And *you* went off to become rich and famous.

BUBBA. I'm big in Waco.

DAISY. No, you're not.

BUBBA. I could be.

HANK. *(To DARLA.)* Money and fame don't really matter if you're not with the one ya love.

DAISY.	**BUFORD.**
(Melting.) Ohh.	*(Groans.)* Ohh.

DARLA. Always the charmer.

BUFORD. A *snake* charmer!

HANK. We had some great times together.

DARLA. Yeah, we did.

HANK. Remember my nickname for you?

DARLA. I sure do, "Catnip."

> *(They both do a cheesy Eskimo kiss with their little cat paws out.)*

HANK & DARLA. Mew, mew, mew, mew, mew, mew, mew.

BUFORD. Stop that, right now!

> *(Laughing, they stop. They both end their laugh at the same time with a big sigh.)*

HANK. Let's do that again.

DARLA. Okay.

(Again, they both do a cheesy Eskimo kiss with their little cat paws out.)

HANK & DARLA. Mew, mew, mew, mew, mew, mew, mew.

BUFORD. Get off her!

*(**HANK** and **DARLA** stop their little kiss with another sigh.)*

*(To **HANK**.)* I will take you out like a tornado in a trailer park!

DARLA. Did ya ever get married?

HANK. I never did.

DAISY. He's available!

HANK. After you left me for that other guy...

BUFORD. Buford.

HANK. I could never find the right woman.

DARLA. Oh, that's a shame. You have so much to offer.

DAISY. So much.

BUFORD. Oh, c'mon!

HANK. I have a confession to make.

DAISY. He has a confession! Hank Walker has a confession!

HANK. I heard about Buford's accident, and, well...all these years I've been hopin' for a chance to win ya back. I just didn't know when to approach ya. I mean, I wanted to be respectful of your marriage and whatnot, and when I heard that Buford was in a coma, well, it just seemed like the appropriate time to come a-knockin'.

DAISY. So romantic.

BUFORD. No, it ain't! It's sick!

HANK. Some might think I'm tryin' to take advantage of somebody else's misfortune.

BUFORD. Well, yeah, by definition!

DARLA. I don't think you are.

BUFORD. Well, what do ya call it?

HANK. I just wanted to stop by, see ya again, and reminisce about the good old days, without Buford bein' here.

DARLA. Well, I'm glad ya did.

BUFORD. *(To* **DARLA.***)* He's tryin' to reel ya in. Don't take the bait.

HANK. It's just that Buford's been a little upset at me.

DARLA. Oh, he'll get over it.

BUFORD. When pigs fly!

HANK. It's just that I didn't wanna create any friction.

DAISY. I wanna create friction.

BUBBA. There will be no friction.

DARLA. Talk about us some more.

BUFORD. What is happenin' here?!

HANK. *(To* **DAISY** *and* **BUBBA.***)* We used to go out dancin' on Saturday night.

    (To **DARLA.***)* Remember?

DARLA. Oh, yeah.

HANK. I loved to dance with Darla.

BUFORD. Don't you dare. I know you can hear me!

HANK. You ever dance with Buford?

DARLA. Nah, he's too manly.

BUFORD. What's wrong with manly?!

HANK. Oh, that's too bad.

    (To **BUBBA** *and* **DAISY.***)* Darla and I competed in the West Texas Dance-a-Palooza.

(To **DARLA**.*)* We sure did tear up that dance floor, didn't we?

DARLA. We sure did.

HANK. Remember our signature move?

DARLA. Of course I do.

HANK. "The dip and kiss."

BUFORD. Is *not* what I wanna hear.

DAISY. Do it for us!

BUFORD. NO!

DARLA. Hank is the best kisser, ever!

BUFORD. Well, *that* seems unnecessary.

HANK. *(Holds his hand out to* **DARLA**.*)* Would you do me the honor, Miss Darla?

BUFORD. No, she would not.

DARLA. Okay.

BUFORD. *(Groans.)* Ohh!

> (**DARLA** *gets up, holding* **HANK***'s hand.)*

HANK. Just as the song was about to begin, we would get in our dance position and hold each other thusly.

> (**HANK** *holds* **DARLA** *close, in their "dance" position.)*

BUFORD. I do not like where this is goin'.

HANK. When the music started we would move back and forth, staring at each other in the face, in a loving manner, like such.

> *(They move back and forth as if they're dancing in place, staring at each other.)*

DAISY. No one ever looked at me like that.

HANK. We were laser-beam focused on each other's eyes. It was like we were one personage. We had a connection. A love connection.

DAISY. I wanna connection!

BUBBA. Hashtag, no connection!

HANK. We took over the dance floor and everybody was watchin' us, wonderin', "What are they gonna do? Are they gonna kiss?" All eyes in the room were fixed on us.

BUFORD. My eyes just barfed.

HANK. It was like rubbin' two sticks together to start a fire, only the sticks were our desirous torsos. The heat between us was palpable.

BUBBA. Now he's just makin' up words.

HANK. As we danced ever so coquettishly...

BUBBA. Not a word.

HANK. ...We would whisper sweet nothin's to each other.

> *(They both mouth sweet nothings to each other, not actually talking, just moving their lips as if they were.)*

DAISY. What are they sayin'?

BUBBA. Nothin'! He just told ya!

HANK. Toward the end of the song, Darla and I would hold each other closely, as I demonstrate, heretofore.

> *(Holding **DARLA** closer.)*

BUFORD. Oh, no, ya don't! Release her!

HANK. Can ya feel the chemistry that's emanatin' right now between our palpitatin' body cavities?

DARLA. Oh, I feel it. I do.

DAISY. I do, too!

BUFORD. I am *not* enjoyin' this.

HANK. After several moments of dancin' pleasure, the music would build to a dramatic crescendo. And when I could no longer contain my emotions inside, I would put my hand behind her feminly back, and then I would dip her, puckishly.

(**HANK** *dips* **DARLA**.)

BUBBA. Alright, that's dirty.

BUFORD. There will be no dippin'!

HANK. And finally, I would go in for the biggest kiss this side of El Paso.

(*To* **DAISY**.) You wanna see it? You wanna see the kiss?

DAISY. Yes, I do!

DARLA. I do, too!

BUFORD. I don't!

BUBBA. I gotta be honest. I got mixed feelin's about the kiss.

HANK. Ya ready? I'm comin' in. Here, I come. I'm gonna do it.

DAISY. Do it!

DARLA. What are ya waitin' for?!

HANK. I'm waitin' for the green light.

DARLA. I am wavin' you in!

HANK. Buckle your seat belt and put up your tray table, 'cause I'm approachin' the runway.

BUFORD. Stay off her tarmac!

HANK. Landin' gear is down! I'm comin' in!

    (In slow motion, **HANK** *moves in to kiss* **DARLA**. **DAISY** *and* **BUBBA** *move in slow motion, cheering them on.)*

BUFORD. Nooooooooooooo!

    (The lights fade to black just as their lips touch.)

ACT TWO

(**DARLA** *clears the final empty plates from the table and sets them on the bar.* **HANK, BUBBA,** *and* **DAISY** *are in chairs, sitting back in a semi-comatose state. They've eaten way too much. Beer bottles are in front of them.* **DAISY** *has a shot glass. She's a little tipsy.*)

HANK. Oh, boy, thanks again for dinner, there, Darla. I am stuffed.

BUBBA. Me, too.

DARLA. I'm really glad ya liked it.

HANK. *(To* **DARLA,** *seductively.)* I just loved your jiblets.

DARLA. *(Laughs.)* Oh, you.

BUFORD. Stay away from her jiblets!

DARLA. Daisy made the appetizers.

HANK. They were so good.

DAISY. When what to my wondering eyes should appear... but ten extra pounds on my hips, thighs and rear.

(**DAISY** *laughs.*)

DARLA. Hey, why don't we all go around and say a little somethin' about Christmas. Maybe a good memory, a thought, whatever comes to mind. What do y'all think? Daisy?

DAISY. Sure, alright, let me think... Oh, okay, here goes, this year, I'm dreaming of a white Christmas, but if it runs out, I'll drink the red.

(**DAISY** *laughs.*)

BUFORD. She went a long way for that one.

BUBBA. I'm dreamin' of a Christmas with Daisy. Sittin' there on the rug in front of our big fireplace, huggin' and kissin', with our six kids and twenty-eight grandchildren...

(*Picturing them.*) There's Little Bubba Junior, Bubbette, Bubba Gump, Bubbalicious, Hubba Bubba –

DAISY. Please stop.

DARLA. I'm dreamin' of a self-cleanin' bathroom.

HANK. (*Waits a beat for more from* **DARLA***, realizes she's done.*) Oh, okay, ahh...I'm just grateful to be part of your little family this year, and to be able to see Darla again.

DAISY. Oh, bless your heart.

BUFORD. Oh, cranberries.

DARLA. That's nice, Hank. Thank you for that.

HANK. Thank *you.*

DAISY. So, Hank, you said you had my fried ham poppers at the Bigfoot Lounge in Amarillo. Do you live there?

HANK. No, I was just visitin'. I know the owner.

DAISY. (*Impressed.*) Oh! Well, I guess you know a lot of restaurant owners cause of your barbecue sauce.

HANK. Yeah, it's part of the business.

DAISY. Do you know any people in the Manhattan?

HANK. *The* Manhattan? Ya mean New York City?

DAISY. Best restaurants in the world. The Bad Apple.

BUBBA. (*Correcting her.*) Actually, I think it's called the Big –

DARLA. Let it go –

BUBBA. Okay.

HANK. Well, I probably know people who know people in the Manhattan.

BUBBA. Alright, Daisy, let's give Hank some air here, okay? It's Christmas. You can talk about business with Hank some other time, like, never.

DAISY. I'm just bein' conversant.

BUBBA. Well, conversant on another topic.

DAISY. Alright. So, Hank, tell us about when ya dated Darla.

BUFORD. Not *that* topic!

HANK. It was the best time of my life.

DAISY. *(How sweet.)* Ohh.

HANK. *(To* **DARLA.***)* Remember when we used to go out to Jepsen's barn?

DARLA. I sure do.

DAISY. Oh, my gosh. How romantic.

BUFORD. Wait, *I* took her to Jepsen's barn.

HANK. *(To* **BUBBA** *and* **DAISY.***)* We used to play Lewis and Clark. I would take Darla over my shoulder, throw her in the hay, and "explore her territory."

DARLA.	**BUFORD.**
Hank!	Okay! Okay!

DAISY. I wanna be explored!

BUBBA. That's it, no more Wild Turkey for *you*!

DAISY. Oh, don't get your tinsel in a tangle. The tree ain't the only thing gettin' lit this year!

BUBBA. Alright, let's just dial it down, there, Miss Tipsy.

    (To **DARLA.***)* Does she have a drinkin' problem?

DAISY. No, she has a drinkin' *solution.*

    *(***DAISY** *laughs.)*

BUFORD. He walked into that one.

HANK. I have another confession to make.

DAISY. He has another confession. Hank has another confession!

BUBBA. *(Gets up to escort* **DAISY** *to the kitchen.)* Alrighty, let's just go ahead and get you some coffee, there. There's a whole pot in the kitchen. You can drink all of it.

    *(***BUBBA** *starts walking* **DAISY** *to the kitchen.)*

DAISY. Oh, you're no fun, Bubba. "Bubba, Bubba, Bubba, Bubba, Bubba, Bubba, Bubba."

    (She puts her index finger on her lips parallel to them, and moves it up and down, making noise.)

B-b-b-b-b-b-b-b-b.

BUBBA. In ya go.

    *(***DAISY** *and* **BUBBA** *exit into the kitchen. As he goes in,* **BUBBA** *grabs the empty plates on the bar and brings them with him.)*

HANK. I've been thinkin' a lot about ya lately, Darla.

DARLA. Really?

BUFORD. I can't listen.

HANK. Yeah, and I just kinda blame myself for lettin' ya get away.

(**BUFORD** *closes his eyes and puts his fingers in his ears, not to hear.*)

BUFORD.	HANK.
(To himself, quietly.) La la la la la la la la la la la la la la la la la la la la la la la la la la la la la.	I know you've always wanted children, and I know about Buford's problem down there.

BUFORD. *(Opening his eyes, taking his fingers out of his ears.)* Does everybody know?!

DARLA. What are ya sayin' there, Hank?

HANK. I just think I could make ya very happy, that's all. Give ya the kids you want. I'm not suggesting you divorce Buford, or nothin'. I mean, I don't think you'll have to... Have ya ever heard of a thing called "do not resuscitate"?

BUFORD. Oh, cheese and crackers.

HANK. I'm just sayin' if ya pull the tubes out, he'll go peacefully.

BUFORD. Don't touch my tubes!

DARLA. I don't know, Hank, it just seems a little early for that, don't ya think? I mean, he's only been in a coma for three hours.

HANK. Well, how long were ya gonna wait?

DARLA. I was thinkin' a day or two.

BUFORD. It's only a dream. It's only a dream.

HANK. Did Buford have life insurance?

DARLA. Nah, too cheap.

BUFORD. I'm self insured, thank you.

HANK. Alright, well, I just want you to know that I'll be there to take care of ya.

(**BUBBA** *enters from the kitchen.*)

DARLA. Yeah, well, I appreciate the offer, there, Hank. And I may take you up on that, too, 'cause…I'm pregnant.

BUFORD.	**BUBBA.**
What?	What?

DARLA. I did the test to make sure. I'm gonna have a baby.

BUBBA. It's a miracle baby!

DARLA. No, it's Buford's.

BUBBA. *(Casually.)* Oh.

BUFORD. *(Doing a victory dance.)* I did it! I did it! Yippee ki yay, I did it, bam!

HANK. The baby will need a father.

DARLA. It has a father.

BUFORD. Me!

HANK. I know, but one that doesn't require a sponge bath.

DARLA. Yeah, good point.

BUFORD. No, it ain't.

HANK. I have a big cabin on Lake Texoma you could live in. You could keep the restaurant, if ya want. Change the name to "Darla's Real Good Barbecue…

(*He thinks.*)

Place." You'd never have to worry about a mortgage payment again.

DARLA. Oh, thanks, Hank, that's very flattering.

BUFORD. Yeah, I'd like to flatter him. With my wood chipper!

(**BUFORD** *mimes pushing* **HANK** *in a wood chipper with sound effects.*)

HANK. All I ask is that ya think about it.

DARLA. I will.

DAISY. *(From the kitchen.)* Pick me! Pick me!

BUBBA. Drink your coffee and behave!

DAISY. I'd rather be naughty!

> *(The kitchen door opens, and* **DAISY** *steps out. She's wearing a sexy Santa outfit.)*

HANK. Holy Fifty Shades of Grey.

BUBBA. Oh, no ya don't. That just ain't gonna happen, alright?

> *(**BUBBA** steps in front of* **DAISY**, *hiding her outfit.)*

DAISY. What are ya doin?

> *(Pushing* **BUBBA** *away from her.)*

BUBBA. That dress ain't decent. That's the kind of thing ya see on that Victoria Secret catalogue centerfold...

> *(Busted, looks at everyone.)* That I do not have duct-taped on my refrigerator.

DARLA. Bubba! Park it!

BUBBA. *(He sits.)* Why is she wearin' that?

DAISY. It's my cookin' show dress. I'm gonna wear it on the TV.

BUBBA. That dress is naughty.

DAISY. That's 'cause I was naughty this year. I mean, I tried to be good, but then I just got bored.

I mean, think about it, one day of coal, three hundred sixty-four days of fun. I'll take my chances.

HANK. Sounds like you're on the naughty list.

BUBBA. Alright, well, since we's on the topic, how were ya naughty? I'm just askin' for research purposes. Be specific.

DAISY. Well, when I'm at the grocery store, I squeeze the fruit and I put it back.

BUBBA. Wow. Your definition of naughty is *way* different than mine.

DAISY. I don't refill the ice trays. I never make my bed. I don't observe Groundhog Day. Should I go on?

HANK. Yeah, I'm not sure you're on the naughty list.

DAISY. Well, how do I get there?

BUBBA. I got this. I can help ya with that. We'll start with the "dip and kiss," and then we'll move on to –

DAISY. Hank, I got a proposition.

BUBBA. I'm invisible.

DAISY. *(Suggestively to* **HANK.***)* If you help me get to the Manhattan, I could help ya sell your barbecue sauce.

HANK. I bet you could.

DAISY. Do one of them tv commercials where I put some of your barbecue sauce on a brisket sandwich, maybe sit on the hood of a Ford F-150, like in those sexy hamburger commercials, bite down on the brisket and get barbecue all over me. Rub a dub dub.

> *(***DAISY*** *mimes eating the sandwich and getting sauce all over her.)*

HANK. You're hired.

BUFORD. Now *this* is entertainment!

BUBBA. *(To* **DAISY.***)* Okay, let's summarize...so, in this commercial that everybody is gonna see, ya sit on the hood of a Ford F-150, all covered in barbecue sauce, writhin' around in your little sexy Santa outfit. Is that about it?

DAISY. Yeah.

BUBBA. *(Sarcastic.)* I am so proud of you.

DAISY. Thanks.

BUBBA. Sarcasm!

DAISY. Oh.

BUBBA. Yeah, okay, so why don't ya just go ahead, there, and forget all about writhin' around in barbecue sauce while ya put on somethin' a little less risk-way.

DAISY. Alright, Bubba, here's the deal… We're not datin' anymore, okay, so ya can't tell me what to do. Not that ya could when we *were* datin', but now ya really can't.

BUBBA. Well, I'm open to givin' it another shot.

DAISY. *(Sarcastic.)* Oh, gosh, well that's tempting.

BUBBA. Really?

DAISY. *(Imitating* **BUBBA.***)* "Sarcasm"!

BUFORD. Oh, snap!

HANK. Daisy, I'd like to sponsor you to go on tour.

DAISY. *(Excited.)* Well, light my candle, that just dills my pickle!

(Changes her tone.) Okay, what kind of tour are we talkin' about?

HANK. A cookin' tour, with a live show where ya get up onstage and cook stuff in front of thousands of adoring fans. Or less.

DAISY. A cookin' tour! Sakes alive. This must be a dream.

BUFORD. In fact, it is.

HANK. And on the tour you can promote my barbecue sauce.

BUFORD. I knew it.

HANK. I know lots of restaurant and bar owners and county fairs that would love to have you do a live cookin' show.

DAISY. Is this for real?

HANK. Well, sure, I think you're good, I really do, but ya know what, ya gotta get out there, ya gotta be seen, 'cause if you're not seen...

(Thinks.) They won't see ya.

DAISY. *(Overly enthusiastic.)* Well, knock me down and steal my teeth!

BUBBA. *(To HANK.)* Alright, let's pump the breaks, there, Talladega!

BUFORD. *(To BUBBA, re: DAISY.)* Let her go!

HANK. And Darla, I'd like you to be my life partner.

BUFORD. Oh, no, ya don't!

BUBBA. Alright, there, Romeo, why don'tcha take a little saltpeter, there.

BUFORD. Yeah.

HANK. I can't help it. It's just that all my emotions inside are comin' out and I just wanna share 'em with you.

DAISY.	**BUFORD.**
(Sighs.) Oh!	*(Groaning.)* Oh!

HANK. Do you like romance?

DARLA. I don't know. I never experienced it.

DAISY. I like romance.

HANK. Well, sure ya do. We all like romance now, don't we?

BUFORD. Speakin' for all men, no.

HANK. If Buford did somethin' romantic for ya, what would ya do?

DARLA. Pass out.

HANK. You'd like it though, wouldn't ya?

DARLA. I can't even visualize it.

HANK. You ever try anything to spice up your relationship? Fantasies or role playin'?

DARLA. I used to pretend that Buford was somebody else.

BUFORD. Oh, for pokin' the bear.

HANK. *(Takes* **DARLA***'s hand.)* Come on, Darla, run away with me, and I will show you sights you have never seen, and give you the love and affection you so rightly deserve. Mon amour.

*(***HANK*** kisses* **DARLA***'s hand.)*

DAISY. That's French. He spoke French. Oh!

HANK. Mais oui, omelette du fromage.

DAISY. Oh!

HANK. With me, the world is your oyster.

DAISY. I love seafood!

HANK. I will spend money on you like you have never seen. I will take you to fancy restaurants with candles and cloth napkins.

DARLA. Hell's bells!

HANK. Where we will order appetizers.

DARLA. Holy moly!

DAISY. Shrimp cocktail!

BUFORD. How can ya compete?

HANK. And you can order anything on the menu even if it says, "market price."

DAISY. I never had, "market price"!

DARLA. I don't even know what that is!

BUFORD. I'm done. Stick a fork in it.

HANK. We'll travel the world, we'll see the sights from Branson, Missouri to Paris…

(To audience.) Texas.

DAISY. So romantic.

HANK. And finally, I will shampoo your hair, and bring you flowers for no reason at all.

DARLA. Oh, my lucky stars!

BUFORD. I'm toast!

HANK. What do ya say, mon aperitif? Let's go, right now. Let's blow this corn dog stand and run away. Just the two of us.

BUFORD. *(To DARLA.)* Don't do it.

DARLA. Oh, my gosh, I just don't know.

DAISY. I'll go!

BUBBA. *(Caught up in it.)* So will I…

(Catches himself.) Wait, no! Alright, Daisy, here's the deal. If ya stay here, I'll give ya fifty thousand dollars for every baby ya have.

DAISY. *(Excited.)* Glory be!

(Then realizes.) Wait, with you?

BUBBA. Yeah, with me.

HANK. Daisy, you're young, you can have babies in a few years when ya get tired of touring, and who knows, maybe ya won't get tired.

BUBBA. Alright, Hank, I'm havin' a conversation with Daisy, here, alright? So, why don't ya just go in that corner over there, and stick your nose in your rump roast.

BUFORD. Yeah!

DAISY. Hank is right, though. I could have babies in a few years.

BUBBA. Yeah, but the offer is only good for thirty days.

DAISY. Bubba, it takes longer than thirty days to have a baby.

BUBBA. I'm sayin' if ya go on tour, the offer is null and void.

HANK. Like your brain.

BUBBA. Yeah...

(Realizing.) No... Wait...

(To **DAISY.***)* Okay, and here's the kicker. I was savin' this one for last... I will build you a booth next to gas station number six and we'll call it, ya ready for this?

(Gesturing a billboard.) "Daisy's Cookin'...

(Thinks.) and then Gas." And you can cook whatever you want.

HANK. If ya go on tour with me, ya won't need...

(Gesturing a billboard, mimicking **BUBBA.***)* "Daisy's Cookin'...and then Gas."

BUBBA. Fifty thousand a baby, *and...*

(Gesturing a billboard.) "Daisy's Cookin'...and then Gas."

HANK. Tour with me and you could get discovered, plus you'll be bringin' in your own dough.

DAISY. If I have my own doe, I could open up a deer-petting farm.

(Everyone looks at each other for a few moments thinking, "Did she really say that?")

HANK. Bless your heart.

BUBBA. He don't mean *that* kinda doe, he means *bakery* dough.

HANK. *(Taking that in for a beat.)* Maybe they *should* be together.

BUBBA. I didn't wanna have to resort to this, but, rock, paper, scissors for Daisy.

> *(He holds out his fist, pumps twice, then does "scissors." **HANK** isn't playing.)*

He ain't doin' it. He knows I'd win.

DARLA. *(To **BUBBA**.)* Dork.

DAISY. Gosh, I don't know. It's just so hard to decide. Fifty thousand a baby plus my own...

(Gesturing a billboard.) "Daisy's Cookin'...and then Gas," or the uncertainty of goin' on tour... What would Dolly Parton do?

> *(**DARLA** lifts up a big photo of Dolly Parton from behind the bar.)*

BUFORD. Oh, just kill me now.

BUBBA. That's the most random thing I have ever seen.

DAISY. No, it isn't. Dolly knows all about touring.

BUBBA. Well, what does she know about food?

DAISY. She has her own cookbook, "Dolly's Dixie Fixin's," and her own theme park. Dolly Parton knows everything!

> *(**BUBBA** goes behind the bar and ducks down below it, putting on a baby bonnet.)*

DARLA. Talk to her, Daisy. She's here for you.

DAISY. Please give me a sign, Dolly. I know you can help me. I mean, we're so much alike, except for you're really rich, and you don't live with your parents in a trailer. Should I go with Bubba or Hank?

HANK. Seems clear to me.

DAISY. I would like two babies, a boy and a girl. But what if they turn out like Bubba?

> (**BUBBA** *pops his head up from behind the bar, wearing a baby bonnet, holding a baby bottle and a rattle.*)

BUBBA. Momma!

DAISY. *(Re:* **BUBBA** *in the baby bonnet.)* Oh, no!

BUBBA. Goo goo, y'all! Pa chow.

DAISY. I will *never* un-see that!

> (**BUBBA** *goes back under the bar and takes off the baby outfit.*)

(To the Dolly Parton photo.) What should I do, Dolly? Have babies with Bubba for fifty thousand dollars or go on tour and cook food in front of thousands of adoring fans? Or less. With a chance to have my own cookin' show on the TV. Tell me now.

> (**BUBBA** *comes up from behind the bar.*)

DARLA. *(Holding the Dolly Parton photo in front of her face, doing her best Dolly impression.)* Go on tour! Seriously. I mean, why would you ever wanna Bubba baby?

(Realizing how funny that sounds, she repeats it.) Bubba baby, Bubba baby...

> (**DAISY** *joins* **DARLA.**)

DAISY & DARLA. Bubba baby, Bubba baby, Bubba baby –

DARLA. Okay, we're gettin' off track, here. I mean, here's the deal. Bubba has the I.Q of a tree frog. I'm surprised he can even dress himself.

BUBBA. I'm standin' right here.

DAISY. Okay, I'll do it! I'll go on tour!

> (**DARLA** *puts the Dolly Parton photo back behind the bar.*)

HANK. Hey, Darla, where'd ya get the photo?

DARLA. *(Casually.)* Behind the bar.

HANK. Oh.

BUBBA. Alright, so, Daisy...what's your decision?

DAISY. Were ya not in the room?

BUBBA. Ya know, if I have to pay attention to everything that's goin' on, here. I mean...

DAISY. I'm goin' on tour with Hank.

BUBBA. Wow. I did *not* see *that* comin'.

HANK. What about you, Darla?

BUFORD. Don't do it.

DARLA. Golly, I just don't know.

HANK. I sure would hate to lose ya again.

> *(Getting emotional.)* I'm sorry, I'm just gettin' a little emotional.

DAISY.	**BUFORD.**
(Swooning.) Ohh!	*(Groans.)* Ohh!

DARLA. Oh, that is so sweet. I mean, it's just so nice to be with somebody who shares his feelin's and can cry.

BUFORD. Oh, for crap sake.

HANK. And what about our kiss? That must have meant somethin' to ya. Our long, slow, kiss, all sloppy, and slurpy and...

(**HANK** *and* **DARLA** *parody their previous kiss with sound effects [without kissing] while* **BUFORD** *watches.*)

BUFORD. Thank you for relivin' that!

DARLA. So romantic... I just need a couple days to think on this one.

HANK. Are ya sure?

DARLA. Yeah.

HANK. Alright, that's fair... Take a couple days and I'll come back then for your decision.

BUFORD. Don't bother!

HANK. *(To* **DARLA.***)* Thank you for dinner.

DARLA. You're welcome.

(**HANK** *hugs* **DARLA** *for a very long time.*)

BUFORD. *(Watching them hug.)* Alright, take it easy.

(*They continue to hug.*)

Okay, ya can just go ahead and stop doin' that.

(*The hug gets more passionate.*)

Sweet blue cheese, would ya break it up!

(*They release their hug.*)

DARLA. I haven't been hugged like that since, ahh...

(**DARLA** *can't think of his name.*)

BUFORD. Buford!

DARLA. Since Buford hugged me on my birthday... And that's only 'cause our belt buckles got stuck together.

HANK. *(Standing at the door.)* Reservoir, mon souffle.

DAISY.   **BUFORD.**

(Swooning.) Ohh!   *(Groaning.)* Ohh!

> *(**HANK** blows **DARLA** a kiss, she catches it. He heads out the door. **DARLA** looks out the window and watches **HANK** leave.)*

BUFORD. *(Looking up.)* Alright, I get it, you're punishin' me. Now, what do I need to do to get this over with?

BUBBA. Well the good news is, Hopalong Skittle-brain is gone. Now Daisy, I know you got a tough decision to make –

DAISY. I'm goin' on tour.

BUBBA. But what about me?

DAISY. Oh, Bubba, we just want different things.

BUBBA. I know, but you'll come around.

DAISY. Listen, Bubba, I'm gonna say somethin' and I want you to completely clear your mind.

BUBBA. *(Quickly.)* Done.

DAISY. You're a good-hearted guy. I mean, I don't have a lot to back that up with. Anyway, I'm sure you'll find the right woman if you're patient and ya lower your standards.

> *(**BUBBA** leans in to kiss her. She leans away.)*

What are you doin'?

BUBBA. I just can't read you sometimes.

DAISY. The point is, I'm just not right for you. What did ya say was the most important quality in a woman?

BUBBA. Would she be a good killin' partner during the zombie apocalypse.

DAISY. Exactly. And that's just not me. You deserve a real woman. I'm talkin' about a woman that can field dress a deer.

(**DAISY** *motions like she's field dressing a deer.*)

BUBBA. Ya know, Daisy, we *was* engaged once.

DAISY. I know, Bubba, and I'm not proud of that time in my life. I mean, I just didn't have a lot of options. What I'm sayin' is you *were* the only single guy in town, and one day I realized...there's a reason for that.

(**DAISY** *starts toward the kitchen.* **BUBBA** *follows her.*)

BUBBA. I keep gettin' these mixed signals from ya.

DAISY. Hey Darla, I'm goin' to the Piggly Wiggly if ya wanna come.

(**BUBBA** *and* **DAISY** *disappear into the kitchen.*)

DARLA. Oh, no, thanks. I think I'm gonna wait to see what happens to, ahh...

(**DARLA** *can't think of his name.*)

BUFORD. Buford.

DARLA. To Buford.

(**DARLA** *goes into the kitchen.*)

BUFORD. I am *not* havin' a good day.

(*He looks up.*)

Any chance I could get a little guidance on this?... Maybe get me outta this dream or somethin'?... Anybody there?... I cannot catch a break.

(**HANK** *comes out of the bathroom, wearing a Grim Reaper robe with a hood over his head, carrying a scythe.*)

HANK. *(Howling like a ghost, pointing at* **BUFORD**.*)* Ooooooooooooooooh.

BUFORD. *(He sees* **HANK** *in his outfit.)* Oh, great, it's the dim reaper.

HANK. No, it's just me.

(**HANK** *pulls the hood off his head.*)

BUFORD. So, what, you can see me now?

HANK. *(Duh.)* Yeah.

BUFORD. Well, ya couldn't a minute ago when you were here with...oh, never mind... Look, I don't wanna do this anymore, alright? Ya made your point.

HANK. Have I? I mean, somethin' tells me you haven't really learned your lesson yet.

BUFORD. I have too. I've been bad, I'll be good from now on, let's just end this thing, alright?

HANK. Can't end it, yet, Krispy Kreme. Ya got one more test, the ghost of Christmas yet to come.

(Making ghost sounds.) Ooooooooooooooooooh.

BUFORD. You're playin' all the ghosts?

HANK. I get time and a half.

BUFORD. Can we just skip this part? I mean, I think I have a pretty good handle on where this rodeo is headin'.

HANK. No can do, Pop-Tart. There are no shortcuts in life.

BUFORD. It's not like I wanna take a shortcut or nothin'. I just wanna quit.

HANK. Just like you quit our barbecue business?

BUFORD. Oh, what are you complainin' about? You took my barbecue sauce and made a ton of money with it.

HANK. "Your" barbecue sauce.

BUFORD. You know it was. Oh, I'm tired of arguin' about it. Let's just get this over with.

HANK. Now *that's* the spirit.

> *(He laughs.)*

Get it? 'Cause I'm a spirit.

(Laughs, then to **BUFORD**.*)* Boo.

BUFORD. You're a moron.

> *(***DARLA** *and* **BUBBA** *come out of the kitchen, wearing matching red plaid shirts.* **BUBBA** *is chewing gum.)*

DARLA. Merry Christmas, Bubba.

BUBBA. Merry Christmas, my lovely wife.

> *(***BUBBA** *kisses* **DARLA**.*)*

BUFORD. She's married to Bubba?!

HANK. That's right.

BUBBA. Eight blissful years. Where does the time go?

DARLA. It's just been one long honeymoon.

> *(***BUBBA** *and* **DARLA** *do a cheesy Eskimo kiss with their little cat paws out.)*

BUBBA & DARLA. Mew, mew, mew, mew, mew, mew, mew.

BUFORD. Son of a nutcracker!... So, what about the baby? Did she have the baby?

> *(***DAISY** *comes out of the kitchen, on her knees, like Tiny Tim, but without the crutch. Her shirt matches* **DARLA** *and* **BUBBA**.*)*

DAISY. *(British accent.)* Mummy, Daddy, when can we open the presents?

BUBBA. Soon, Tiny.

BUFORD. He doesn't need a crutch, anymore. That's good.

DAISY. Has anyone seen my crutch?

>   (**BUBBA** *looks behind the bar.*)

BUBBA. Here it is. And we don't call it a crutch, Tiny. It's called "beer."

>   (*From behind the bar,* **BUBBA** *brings out a mug of beer. He hands the beer to* **DAISY.**)

DARLA. Honey, I just don't think Tiny should drink at such a young age.

BUBBA. Oh, it's non-alcoholic.

>   (**BUBBA** *gives* **DAISY** *an exaggerated wink.* **DAISY** *winks back.*)

DARLA. Oh, you.

>   (**BUBBA** *and* **DARLA** *watch as* **DAISY** *chugs the whole beer. She finishes.*)

DAISY. *(Channeling Oliver Twist.)* Please, sir, may I have some more?

BUFORD. Why does the fruit of my loins speak with a British accent?

HANK. Homeschoolin'.

BUBBA. Hey, Darla, would it be okay with you if we did somethin' with Buford's ashes. I mean, they's startin' to creep me out.

>   (**BUBBA** *grabs a Folgers coffee can from behind the bar and puts it on the bar.*)

DARLA. Yeah, you're probably right.

BUFORD. I'm in a coffee can?

BUBBA. Ya made a good choice, there, goin' with the economy urn.

BUFORD. It's Folgers!

HANK. Well, it is the richest kind.

DARLA. That's the way he wanted it. He was just so darn cheap... Hey, why don't we go out and sprinkle him around the parking lot?

BUBBA. Why, is the dumpster full?

BUFORD. *(Groans.)* Ohh!

DAISY. I think we should sprinkle him in the lake.

BUBBA. That's a great idea! That way we can use him for chum. Maybe we'll catch a bass.

DARLA. I think if we're gonna do that, we should at least have a memorial service for him, don't ya think?

DAISY. Didn't ya have one when he died?

BUBBA. Yeah, but no one showed up.

BUFORD. *(To* **HANK.***)* No one?

DAISY. I think we should sing a song.

DARLA. Yeah. We'll sing a song for Buford just like he used to sing to me.

BUBBA. Oh, hey, I got a song. It's perfect.

BUFORD. This can't be good.

DARLA. Alright, well, then, Bubba, why don't you go ahead, there, and start us off.

(**DARLA** *moves a barstool downstage center.*)

BUBBA. Okay...umm...wait a second. Gotta get rid of my gum.

(**BUBBA** *opens the coffee can lid and spits his gum in the can. Ashes fly up from the can.*)

(*He shuts it, then sets the can down on the barstool downstage center.*)

BUBBA. Alright...we's gathered here today...

(**HANK** *begins to "lay down a beat."*)

(*Rapping to* **HANK**'s *beat.*)

YO, YO, YO, LISTEN UP, LISTEN UP. IT'S BUFORD IN DA HOUSE.

DAISY.
WHATCHU MEAN, HE'S IN DA CAN.

BUBBA.
HE WORKED ALL DAY.

DAISY.
WAS AN ANGRY MAN.

BUBBA.
AND THEN ONE DAY.

DAISY.
HE TOOK OFF IN HIS TRUCK.

DARLA. (*Sung to "God Rest Ye Merry Gentlemen."*)
IT'S NOT A BUSY DAY WHEN YOU HAVE NO ONE COMING IN.

BUBBA. (*Rapping.*)
AND ON THAT DAY.

DAISY.
OFF THE ROAD, WITH A CRASH.

BUBBA.
NOW HE'S SITTIN' IN A JOINT.

DAISY.
IN A CAN OF ASH. WICKA.

BUBBA.
> CAN OF ASH.

DAISY.
> WICKA.

DARLA.
> CAN OF ASH.

BUBBA.
> HE SAVED ALL HIS MONEY.

DAISY.
> WAS TIGHTER THAN A FROG'S...

BUBBA.
> ...TWEET!

DAISY.
> WHEN HE PAID YOU A COMPLIMENT.

BUBBA.
> HE ASKED FOR A RECEIPT.

DAISY.
> ASKED FOR A RECEIPT.

DARLA. *(Sung to "March of the Three Kings.")*
> HE'S SO CHEAP, HE WASHED HIS PAPER PLATES. HE
>> STOPPED HIS WATCH SO HE COULD SAVE SOME TIME.

BUBBA. *(Rapping.)*
> HE WON'T EVEN TIP HIS HAT.

DAISY.
> NEVER MADE A TOLL CALL.

BUBBA.
> HE QUIT PLAYIN' GOLF.

DAISY.
> WHEN HE LOST HIS BALL.

BUBBA.
> AND NOW HE'S IN A CAN.

DAISY.

LIKE AN OLD CHEAPSKATE.

BUBBA.

WRITTEN ON HIS EPITAPH.

DAISY.

"I AM NOW FISH BAIT." WICKA.

DARLA.

NOW FISH BAIT.

DAISY.

WICKA.

BUBBA.

NOW FISH BAIT.

DARLA. *(Sung to "Deck the Halls.")*

HE NEVER BOUGHT ME FLOWERS IN HIS LIFE, FA LA LA LA LA LA LA LA...LA LA LA LA LA LA LA LA LA.

BUBBA. *(Rapping.)*

HE LIKED TO TAKE THE TRUCK.

DAISY.

SO HE COULD BE ALONE.

BUBBA.

HE DIDN'T GO TO CHURCH.

DAISY.

NEVER DID ATONE.

BUBBA.

HE DIDN'T LIKE TO HUG.

DAISY.

"DON'T YOU CROSS THE BUBBLE."

BUBBA.

IF YA GET TOO CLOSE.

DAISY.

YA GONNA ASK FOR TROUBLE.

DARLA. *(Sung to "Jingle Bells.")*
BUFORD LOVED ME, LOVED ME SO MUCH, THAT HE
ALMOST TOLD ME.
ALMOST TOLD ME, ALMOST TOLD ME, ALMOST TOLD ME.
YEAH.

BUBBA.
HE DIED A BITTER MAN.

DAISY.
IT DIDN'T HAVE TO BE.

BUBBA.
HIS STORY DIDN'T CHANGE.

DAISY.
HE'S STUCK ON CHAPTER THREE.

BUBBA.
HE NEVER LEARNED THE LESSON.

DAISY.
LIVED IN JEALOUS RAGE.

BUBBA.
YO, IF THE CHAPTER'S BAD.

BUBBA & DAISY.
YA GOTTA TURN THE PAGE.

DARLA. Word.

> *(**DARLA** puts the barstool back by the bar and
> hands **DAISY** the Folgers can. **DAISY**, **BUBBA**,
> and **DARLA** head toward the door.)*

BUFORD. *(Dumbstruck by the absurd song.)* Well, *that* just
happened.

DAISY. Can I pour him in the lake, Mummy?

DARLA. Sure, honey. Just don't get any on ya. Save him for
the fish.

DAISY. Mummy, why is the can warm?

DARLA. Because it's hot where Buford is goin'... You ready?

DAISY. Uh-huh.

> (**DARLA** *on one side of* **DAISY** *and* **BUBBA** *on the other try to lift* **DAISY** *by the arms to carry her out the door. They struggle and can't lift her.*)

Oh, Dumbledore.

> (**DAISY** *stands up and walks out the front door.* **DARLA** *and* **BUBBA** *are stunned.*)

BUBBA. It's a miracle!

DARLA. It's a *Christmas* miracle!

> (**DARLA** *and* **BUBBA** *follow* **DAISY** *out the door.*)

BUFORD. Make it end, okay? I get it, alright? I get it. I'll never be angry again, and I'll start spendin' mo...

> (*He can't say it.*)

Spendin' mo...

> (*He takes a deep breath.*)

I'll start spendin' money. Oh, that hurts.

HANK. How bad do you want it?

BUFORD. I want it, alright? I learned my lesson and I want another chance. Please, just make it end. I can't take it anymore. Spirit, hear. I am not the man I was. Why show me this, if I am past all hope?

(*On his knees, begging.*) Please, I beseech thee! Make it end! Please!

HANK. Doesn't sound very sincere.

BUFORD. (*Getting up.*) Well, then what do I have to do to convince ya?

HANK. You have to say the Pledge of Lady Redemption.

> (**HANK** *hands* **BUFORD** *a piece of paper.* **BUFORD** *looks at it.*)

BUFORD. What in the Frito pie is this?

HANK. The Pledge of Lady Redemption. I just said.

BUFORD. *(Reads a little of the pledge.)* I'm not gonna read that.

> (**BUFORD** *holds the pledge out to* **HANK.**)

HANK. Well, I guess ya don't wanna go back, then.

BUFORD. This is not an appropriate pledge.

HANK. *(To audience.)* Has anything we've done been appropriate?

BUFORD. Pick somethin' else.

HANK. Nope. It has to be the Pledge of Lady Redemption, and it has to be sincere or it doesn't count.

> (**BUFORD** *doesn't respond.*)

Look, Buford, you need to decide what's more important, bein' angry at me or keepin' your wife.

BUFORD. Well, I do enjoy bein' passive-aggressively angry at you.

HANK. It's simple, Buford. If you don't read the pledge, you don't go back. Now, what's it gonna be?

BUFORD. Fine. I'll read it.

> (**BUFORD** *starts to read the pledge to himself, moving his lips as he reads.*)

HANK. Out loud.

BUFORD. *(Reluctantly reads.)* "I acknowledge that, as a man, I have flaws."

(BUFORD looks up at HANK.)

HANK. Keep goin'.

BUFORD. *(Continues to read.)* "But the good news is that I can be redeemed. Because since I have both X and Y chromosomes, it means that I am part woman."

(To HANK.) This is just wrong.

HANK. Ya wanna live or not?

BUFORD. "And because of my superior woman qualities, I have an opportunity to be a better person."

(To HANK.) Who wrote this?

HANK. Darla.

(HANK gestures for BUFORD to keep reading.)

BUFORD. "So today I pledge that I will hug my wife, even if I just hugged her last month. I will hold her hand in public, I will ask her about her day, and I will listen."

(To HANK.) This is lady porn.

HANK. Keep goin'.

BUFORD. *(Continues to read.)* "I will bring her flowers for no reason. I will remember her birthday, anniversary and all major holidays. I will give her greeting cards, sign them, and not return them.

And I will never criticize her life choices because I am one of them."

(BUFORD looks at HANK.)

HANK. Go on.

BUFORD. *(Reads.)* "I pledge that I will tone down my macho stuff, and that I will get in touch with my feminine side."

(Groans.)

Ah..."I will compliment her on a regular basis, and I will get along with her mother."

(*To* **HANK**.) Okay, *that's* not gonna happen.

HANK. It's gotta happen or ya don't go back.

BUFORD. You don't know her mother!

HANK. Keep readin', you're almost done.

BUFORD. (*Reads.*) "I will share my feelin's, be understanding and emotionally available...

(*Groans.*) Ahh. And finally, I pledge that I will tell my wife that I lll...that I lll...

HANK. I'm sorry, tell her what?

BUFORD. Of course I love her. She's out of my league, I know that, and I live in fear every day that I'm gonna lose her.

HANK. Then tell her.

BUFORD. (*Contemplates that.*) Okay, so I read the pledge, so I'm gonna live, then, right?

HANK. I just said you'd go back if ya read it. Whether ya live or not is up to you.

> (*He makes ghost sounds while walking backward to the bathroom.*)

Oooooooooooooooooooooooh. Hank out.

> (**HANK** *exits into the bathroom.* **DARLA** *enters from the front door.*)

BUFORD. Darla! Hey, I'm back! I'm alive! See?

> (**DARLA** *goes behind the bar and starts to clean up. She can't hear* **BUFORD**.)

Darla, I'm right here. I'm okay... Darla?... Darla?... She can't hear me... I've been punked!... He made me say that stupid pledge for nothin'!

HANK. *(Popping his head out of the bathroom.)* Correct.

>*(**HANK** goes back into the bathroom.)*

>*(**DAISY** enters from the front door.)*

DAISY. Hey, Darla, you alright?

DARLA. Yeah, I'm fine.

DAISY. You wanna go visit Buford?

DARLA. I was just there a little while ago.

DAISY. How was he?

DARLA. Still the same. No improvement.

DAISY. I'm sorry.

DARLA. It's just so hard for me to see him like that. I don't know if I can keep doin' it.

DAISY. Well, ya can't give up on him.

DARLA. I just feel so helpless. I don't know what to do. I don't know how to get him back.

BUFORD. I'm right here.

DAISY. It's outta your hands, hon.

DARLA. I just wish there was somethin' I could do.

DAISY. Talk to him. That's what he needs right now, to hear your voice.

DARLA. *(Thinks.)* Could you give me a minute?

DAISY. I'll be in the car. Take your time.

>*(**DAISY** exits. **DARLA** goes behind the bar and takes a drink from her coffee cup.)*

BUFORD. Oh, come on, Darla. Come on, if you could just hear me, I'm right here. I just…

>*(He looks up.)*

Okay, alright, you win. That's right, you win... Alright, look, I know what the deal is, okay? I know it's been awhile since I've been to church...since eighth grade... and, well, I probably have some room for improvement in some areas.

HANK. *(Offstage, sounding God-like.)* In a lot of areas.

BUFORD. Alright, a lot of areas... Sounded like Hank.

HANK. *(Popping his head in from the bathroom.)* It's the holidays, I need the overtime.

   *(**HANK** goes back in the bathroom.)*

BUFORD. *(Looking up.)* Anyway, I'm sorry, alright? I just want it to be like it was when we first met. Ya know, when we were happy. And if you can see it in your heart to forgive me, I promise to be a better person.

   *(Goes to **DARLA**.)* Darla, I promise. I really do.

   *(**DARLA** takes a photo of herself and **BUFORD** off the wall and looks at it.)*

DARLA. I remember when we first met.

BUFORD. It was at Jake's Bar.

DARLA. You were with your friends and you were laughin' about somethin'.

BUFORD. They bet me I wouldn't go over and talk to you.

DARLA. I walked by and you looked over at me.

BUFORD. You were the purtiest thing I ever saw.

DARLA. When you walked up to me, I knew I was in trouble.

BUFORD. I was so nervous.

DARLA. I remember the first thing you said to me.

BUFORD. Oh, no.

DARLA. You said, "Are you an angel? 'Cause it sure smells like somebody died."

(**DARLA** *laughs.*)

BUFORD. That was not my best work.

DARLA. We had such a great time that night, talkin', laughin'.

BUFORD. I fell in love with you the first time I saw ya.

DARLA. That was the happiest I ever was.

BUFORD. From that point on, everything I did was for you.

DARLA. Before I knew it, you proposed to me.

BUFORD. I sure did.

DARLA. In the parking lot at Walmart.

BUFORD. Yeah, I didn't really think that one through.

DARLA. At least your heart was in the right place.

BUFORD. Always for you, Darla.

DARLA. It's not like it used to be, is it? We just don't talk or laugh anymore.

BUFORD. We can get it back, I know we can. It'll be just like it was before, I promise.

DARLA. The doctor said I might have to make a tough decision.

(Emotional.) Why did you do this to me, Buford? I don't know what I'm gonna do. I'm so scared.

BUFORD. Don't be scared, Darla. I'm gonna be okay. I'm feelin' better already.

DARLA. I need you to come back to me.

BUFORD. I will. I promise.

DARLA. *(Tearing up.)* If you don't come back to me...I'm afraid I'm gonna have to let you go.

(**DARLA** *puts the photo back on the wall and heads for the door.*)

BUFORD. No, Darla, don't leave me. Don't give up on me. Come on, Darla, I can't live without ya, okay? I just... I'm sorry, okay? If ya could just please forgive me. I'll do anything.

>   (**DARLA** *opens the door to leave.*)

I love you.

>   (**DARLA** *stops, looks back, thought she heard something. No one there. She exits.*)

No, don't leave me. I'm sorry...

(As he sadly goes into the bathroom.) I did this. It was my fault. It was all my fault.

>   (**BUFORD** *exits. At that moment, the lights flicker and a strange, dreamlike sound is heard.* **BUBBA**, **DAISY**, *and* **DARLA** *enter the front door.*)

DAISY. Darla, I'm sorry about Buford.

DARLA. *(To* **DAISY**.*)* Thanks for bein' there, for me. I really appreciate that.

BUBBA. Well, I'm a giver. It's the least I could do.

DAISY. You are somethin' else, Bubba.

BUBBA. And so was Buford. He'll be remembered as a good man.

DAISY. There's still a chance, Bubba.

BUBBA. Yeah, I know. And I'm gonna win the lotto.

DAISY. Bubba!... Are you brain dead?

BUBBA. No more than Buford.

DAISY. *(Groans.)* Ohh!

BUBBA. Did Buford have a living will?

DAISY. Okay, stop. Bubba, you are proof that evolution can go in reverse.

*(Just then, **BUFORD** enters from the front door, wearing the same thing he wore at the beginning, carrying a plastic garbage bag. Everyone looks at him, wide-eyed. **BUFORD** looks around.)*

BUFORD. If this is Heaven, I have been misled.

*(**BUFORD** sets the bag down.)*

DARLA. Buford?!

DAISY. Oh, my gosh. It's Buford! He's okay!

BUBBA. Beers on the house!

*(**BUBBA** goes to get himself a beer.)*

BUFORD. You can see me?!

DARLA. I was so worried.

BUFORD. I'm not dreamin' this?

DARLA. No. Are you okay? How do ya feel?

*(**DARLA** puts her hand to **BUFORD**'s forehead to check.)*

BUFORD. I'm fine. I'm fine. I just... Alright, pinch me just to make sure...

*(**DARLA** pinches **BUFORD** a little too hard.)*

Ah! I'm not dreamin'!

DARLA. It's not a dream, Buford.

BUFORD. What day is it?

DARLA. It's Christmas Day.

BUFORD. It's Christmas Day. It's Christmas Day!

DARLA. Buford, you were in a coma. You almost died. Are ya sure you're okay? Maybe you should go back to the hospital.

BUFORD. No, I'm fine, really, I am. It's just that...I had the weirdest dream.

(To **DARLA**, *à la* The Wizard of Oz.*) You* were there...

(To **DAISY**.*)* and *you* were there...

(To **BUBBA**.*)* and *you're* an idiot.

BUBBA. Well, what was the dream about?

BUFORD. Well, you were married to Darla.

BUBBA. Really? Did we...ya know...pa chow.

BUFORD. Ignorin' that... And all y'all were in the restaurant havin' fun without me.

DAISY. Are you kiddin'? Darla's been in the hospital the whole time. She never left your side. The only reason she's here is 'cause we made her take a break.

BUFORD. Really?

DARLA. I was just so worried.

BUBBA. We just saw ya. You was just in a coma. How in the tater tots did ya get back here so fast?

BUFORD. Oh, yeah, ah, I woke up, they said you just left, and Doc Larson gave me a ride in his pickup. Took a shortcut across Willow Creek.

BUBBA. Oh, right back up on the ol' horse.

BUFORD. Hey, let's all have a great Christmas, alright? Daisy, you can have your job back, if ya want.

DAISY. Thanks!

BUFORD. We'll put your appetizers on the menu, Daisy's fried ham poppers.

DAISY. Oh, my gosh! Thank you so much!

BUFORD. *(Re: her sexy Santa outfit.)* Oh, and I have an idea for a new outfit I'd like ya to try out.

DAISY. Okay.

BUFORD. And Bubba?

BUBBA. *(Hopeful.)* Yeah?

BUFORD. *(Thinks but can't come up with anything.)* Lemme get back to you on that...and Darla...

> *(He grabs the bag, opens it, takes out some flowers, and hands them to* **DARLA.***)*

These are for you. They're fake, but it's a start.

DARLA. Thank you.

BUFORD. I got 'em at the hospital gift shop. Paid full retail.

DARLA. Oh, you are so sweet.

BUFORD. What do you think about changin' the name of the restaurant to,

> *(Gesturing a billboard.)* "Darla's Real Good Barbecue...

> *(Thinks.)* Place."

BUBBA. *(Gesturing a billboard.)* "And then Gas."

DARLA. Yeah, ahh... Why don't we just keep it the way it is.

BUFORD. I'm sorry I've been such an idiot.

DARLA. Oh, that's okay, Buford. I'm just glad you're back.

BUFORD. What do ya think about adopting? We can go find that little Tiny kid. He's probably all grown up and in prison but whatever.

DARLA. *(No idea what he's talking about.)* Yeah, ah, Buford, there's somethin' I wanna tell ya about that... We're gonna have a baby.

BUFORD. For real?! It's not a dream baby?!

DARLA. I just took the test. You're gonna be a daddy.

BUBBA. Score one for the tadpoles!

> (**BUBBA** *takes a drink.*)

BUFORD. (*Looking up, getting emotional.*) Thank you.

HANK. (*Offstage, sounding God-like.*) You're welcome.

> (*Everyone looks around the bar.* **BUFORD** *is tearing up.*)

DARLA. Are you cryin'?

BUFORD. What, *no*! I'm just...sweatin' outta my eyeballs.

DARLA. Alright.

BUFORD. Is it too late to go to Mass?

DARLA. We're Lutheran. We don't have Mass.

BUFORD. Well, whatever we have.

DARLA. Yeah, we can go.

BUFORD. You mean the world to me, Darla. I was wrong to act like such a jerk and I'm sorry. I don't know what I'd ever do without ya. You are the light of my life. And you are the purtiest thing I have ever seen.

DARLA. Oh, stop.

BUFORD. Alright.

DARLA. No, keep goin'.

BUFORD. I love you.

> (**BUBBA** *and* **DAISY** *gasp. They've never heard* **BUFORD** *say that.* **DARLA** *is taken aback.*)

DARLA. I'm sorry, I think I missed that. What did you say?

BUFORD. I love you.

(*BUBBA* and *DAISY* *gasp again.*)

DARLA. (*Puts her hand on his forehead.*) Are you dyin'?

BUFORD. I don't think so.

DARLA. Alright, ahh...

(*Thinks.*) How about one more time. It may be awhile before I hear that again.

BUFORD. I...love...you.

(*BUBBA* and *DAISY* *gasp again.*)

DARLA. I love you too, Buford.

(*They kiss.*)

DAISY. Oh, they're perfect together.

BUBBA. Like whiskey and hunting.

(*BUFORD* and *DARLA* *do a cheesy Eskimo kiss with their little cat paws out.*)

BUFORD & DARLA. Mew, mew, mew, mew, mew, mew, mew.

DAISY. Oh, I think I'm gonna cry.

BUBBA. I think I just threw up in my mouth a little.

(*HANK* *enters, wearing normal street clothes. He looks like a dork, not the sophisticated* *HANK* *with the tuxedo.* *BUFORD* *and* *DARLA* *break the kiss.*)

HANK. Merry Christmas, all y'all.

DAISY. Oh, my gosh. It's Hank Walker! The barbecue king!

BUBBA. (*Not to be outdone.*) I can drive a stick shift.

HANK. Buford, Darla! It's great to see ya! What has it been? Fifteen years?

BUFORD. (*To DARLA.*) You haven't seen him in fifteen years?

DARLA. No.

HANK. Sorry to just barge in on ya. I was in the area, so I just thought I'd stop by, say howdy, and wish y'all a Merry Christmas.

DAISY. Oh, that is so nice.

DARLA. *(To* **HANK.***)* After all these years, you haven't changed a bit.

HANK. I've been doin' the pilates.

BUBBA. *(Bragging.)* I invented the pilates.

DAISY. No, you didn't.

BUBBA. Okay, would ya just let me have *one* thing!

HANK. Oh, Darla, you sure are a vision. As purty as ever.

BUFORD. Oh, it's startin' all over.

HANK. How do ya stay so young?

DARLA. Oh, I don't know.

> *(She hugs* **BUFORD.***)*

It's easy when you're in love.

HANK. You're a lucky guy, there, Buford.

BUFORD. Yeah, I know.

HANK. *(He hands* **BUFORD** *an envelope.)* Merry Christmas.

BUFORD. What's this?

> *(***BUFORD** *opens it.)*

HANK. Fifteen years of royalties for the barbecue sauce. Plus interest.

BUFORD. I'll be hog wallered... Wait, why now?

HANK. Last night I had the weirdest dream.

> *(To* **BUFORD,** *à la* The Wizard of Oz.*)* And *you* were there.

HANK. *(To* DARLA.*)* And *you* were there – Anyway...I just felt so guilty. I'm sorry I didn't pay ya sooner.

BUFORD. *(Looking at the check.)* Whoa!

> *(*BUFORD *shows it to* DARLA.*)*

DARLA. That'll pay off the mortgage!

BUFORD. *(Sincere.)* Yeah, umm, Hank...this is real nice of ya, and everything, but...I'm afraid I just can't accept it...

> *(He starts to hand the check to* HANK*, who starts to reach for it.* BUFORD *quickly pulls it back, laughing.)*

I'm sorry. I just wanted to see if the words would come out of my mouth.

HANK. It's yours, Buford. You deserve it. And the recipe is in there, too. Don't lose it this time.

DARLA. In all my born days!

BUFORD. Thank you.

> *(They shake hands.)*

DAISY. *(With a British accent, channeling Tiny Tim.)* God bless us, everyone!

> *(Everyone looks at* DAISY *for a few beats. Even* DAISY *is confused by her British accent.)*

HANK. *(Turns to* DAISY.*)* Daisy Newsom.

DAISY. That's me. That's *my* name!

BUBBA. He's like a heat-seekin' missile.

HANK. I hear you're a good cook.

BUBBA. Oh, crap.

HANK. And I wanted to ask ya... I'm openin' a restaurant in Amarillo and I was wonderin' if you'd like to be my sous chef.

DAISY. Shut the front door!

> *(Everyone looks at the front door to see if it's open. It's not.)*

HANK. Is that a "yes"?

DAISY. Yes!

> *(**DAISY** hugs **HANK**.)*

BUBBA. *(Up to Heaven.)* Can I please get one break? That's all I'm askin' for.

DAISY. Alright, Bubba. Where's the mistletoe?

BUBBA. *(Quickly pulling mistletoe from his pocket.)* Here ya go.

> *(He holds it over his head.)*

Does this mean we's gonna kiss?

DAISY. Merry Christmas.

BUBBA. Wait... Is this just a sympathy kiss 'cause ya feel sorry for me?

DAISY. Yeah.

BUBBA. I'm okay with that.

> *(**BUBBA** tosses the mistletoe, dips **DAISY**, and kisses her.)*
>
> *(**BUFORD**, **DARLA**, and **HANK** start singing. **BUBBA** is still kissing **DAISY**. Eventually they break the kiss and join in the singing.)*

ALL.

    WE WISH YOU A MERRY CHRISTMAS,
    WE WISH YOU A MERRY CHRISTMAS,
    WE WISH YOU A MERRY CHRISTMAS,
    AND A HAPPY NEW YEAR!

Sure 'nuff, y'all!

    (They all hold two hands out like they're shooting two revolvers.)

Pa chow.

    (Curtain.)

End of Play

PROPS & COSTUMES

ACT ONE

FURNITURE
2 tables (30-36-inch diameter) (stage right, stage left)
4 chairs without arm rests (right and left of each table)
bar (6-8 feet, depending on size of set)
2 barstools

PROPS

on tables:
2 checkered table cloths
2 restaurant napkin holders with napkins
2 sets of salt and pepper shakers
4 food menus (2 on each table)

on bar:
deck of cards dealt out for Buford & Bubba's Gin game
2 beer bottles for Buford & Bubba
Note: Dark beer bottles are best to use with water inside

on floor under Christmas tree:
Christmas tree with ornaments and lights on it (stage left)
additional ornaments in a box by the tree
wrapped Christmas presents under the tree
engagement ring box (unwrapped) under the tree for Bubba
Christmas card (Buford gives it to Darla)

on walls:
Texas beer signs
stuffed fish and various other stuffed animals
Christmas lights and decorations
photo of Buford and Darla behind the bar

behind bar:
liquor bottles
sports trophies
beer tower
beer (preferably non-alcoholic)

underneath bar (items come out during play):
6 beer bottles
2 bar towels
serving tray

in kitchen:
hat with mistletoe hanging from it (Bubba brings it in)
Tiny Tim crutch with outfit (Daisy brings it in)

in bathroom:
fake beard (Bubba brings it in)
Scotch glass with Scotch (tea – Hank brings it in)
tiny chain (Hank brings it in)

other props:
small ghost of Christmas past chain (Hank brings it in)
cookie tin with "fried ham poppers" or equivalent (Daisy brings it in)
piece of scratch paper with joke (Bubba brings it in)
cell phone (Bubba brings it in)
business card (Bubba brings it in)
mail with envelopes (Darla brings it in)

ACT TWO

PROPS

on tables:
4 plates (2 on each table) with food remains with silverwear
assorted beer bottles
shot glass for Daisy on her table

in kitchen:
Sexy Santa outfit – Daisy changes into it
Red plaid shirts – Darla, Bubba, and Daisy/Tiny change into them

on top of bar:
beer bottles

under/behind bar:
large Folgers coffee can with baby powder in it (Bubba takes it out)
poster of Dolly Parton
giant baby bottle, a rattle, and baby bonnet for Bubba
4 beer bottles
mug of beer (preferably non-alcoholic) for Daisy/Tiny
coffee cup for Darla

other props:
mail (envelopes) (Darla brings them in)
chewing gum (Bubba brings it in)
piece of paper – "Pledge of Lady Redemption (Hank brings it in)
mistletoe (Bubba brings it in)
fake flowers in garbage bag (Buford brings it in)

envelope with a check in it (Hank brings it in during last scene)
Grim Reaper robe and scythe (Hank brings them in)

COSTUMES

The costumes reflect what people wear in a small West Texas town: jeans, boots, plaid shirt or work shirt, maybe a cowboy hat. Hank wears a tuxedo when he enters, then changes into a typical West Texas outfit in the last scene.

ACT ONE

– Buford changes into a hospital gown with an Ace bandage around his head.

– Daisy changes into a "Tiny Tim" outfit with boots on her knees, a hat, and a crutch during the Ghost of Christmas Past.

– Darla changes into a different shirt during the Ghost of Christmas Past.

– Bubba puts on a fake beard during the Ghost of Christmas Past.

ACT TWO

– Darla, Bubba, and Daisy/Tiny change into a red plaid shirt in the Ghost of Christmas Yet to Come.

– Hank puts on a Grim Reaper robe with a scythe.

– Hank changes back into normal street clothes in the last scene.

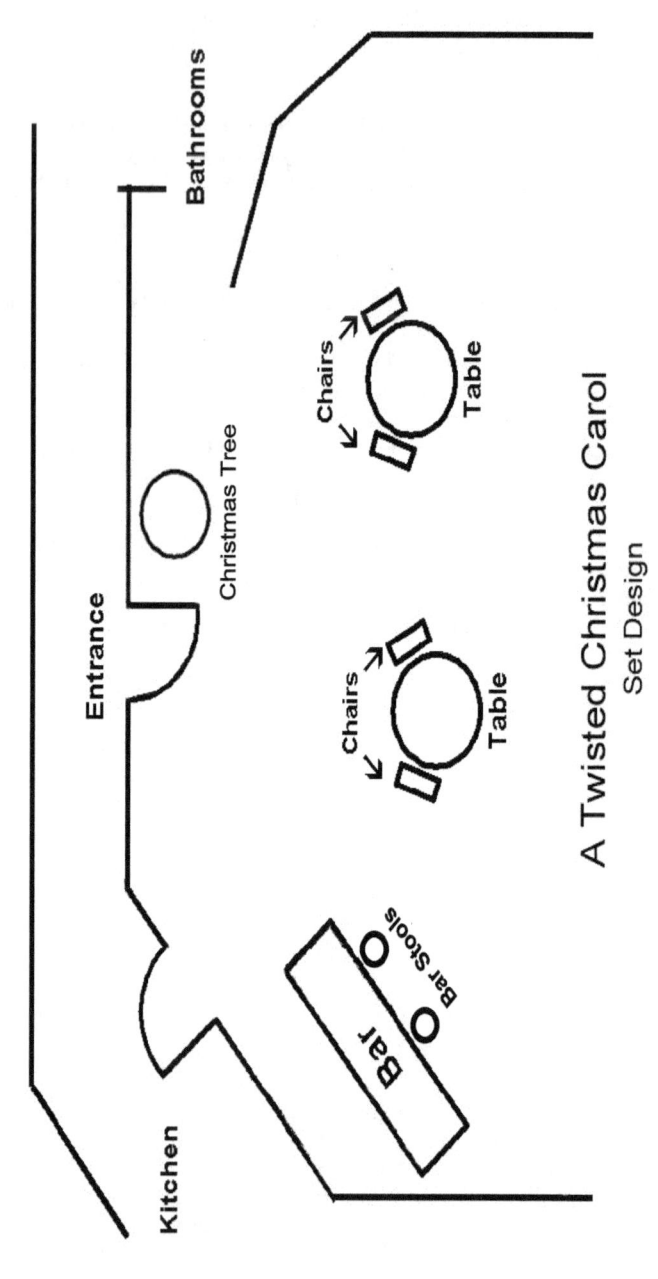

A Twisted Christmas Carol
Set Design

www.ingramcontent.com/pod-product-compliance
Lightning Source LLC
Chambersburg PA
CBHW070334120726
47909CB00008B/2695